THE
PROFESSIONAL
AUNT

Mary C. E. Wemyss

1st WORLD
LIBRARY
Literary Society

The Professional Aunt

Mary C.E. Wemyss

© 1st World Library, 2006
PO Box 2211
Fairfield, IA 52556
www.1stworldlibrary.com
First Edition

LCCN: 2006938095

Softcover ISBN: 978-1-4218-3388-0
Hardcover ISBN: 978-1-4218-3288-3
eBook ISBN: 978-1-4218-3488-7

Purchase *"The Professional Aunt"*
as a traditional bound book at:
www.1stWorldLibrary.com/purchase.asp?ISBN=978-1-4218-3388-0

1st World Library Literary Society

Giving Back to the World

"If you want to work on the core problem, it's early school literacy."

- James Barksdale, former CEO of Netscape

"No skill is more crucial to the future of a child, or to a democratic and prosperous society, than literacy."

- Los Angeles Times

Literacy... means far more than learning how to read and write... The aim is to transmit... knowledge and promote social participation."

- UNESCO

"Literacy is not a luxury, it is a right and a responsibility. If our world is to meet the challenges of the twenty-first century we must harness the energy and creativity of all our citizens."

- President Bill Clinton

"Parents should be encouraged to read to their children, and teachers should be equipped with all available techniques for teaching literacy, so the varying needs and capacities of individual kids can be taken into account."

- Hugh Mackay

CHAPTER I

A boy's profession is not infrequently chosen for him by his parents, which perhaps accounts for the curious fact that the shrewd, business-like member of a family often becomes a painter, while the artistic, unpractical one becomes a member of the Stock Exchange, in course of time, naturally.

My profession was forced upon me, to begin with, by my sisters-in-law, and in the subsequent and natural order of things by their children—my nephews and nieces.

Zerlina says it is the duty of one woman in every family to be an aunt. By that she means of course a professional aunt. She says she does not understand the longing on the part of unattached females—the expression is hers, not mine—for a larger sphere of usefulness than that which aunt hood offers. She considers that it affords full scope for the energies of any reasonably constituted woman; and no doubt, if the professional aunt was all that Zerlina says she should be, she would have her time fully occupied in the discharging of her duties.

Zerlina cannot see that it is not exactly a position of a woman's own choosing, although under strong pressure she has been known to admit that there have been cases in which women have been made aunts whether they would or no; and she thinks it is perhaps by way of protest against such usage that they so shamefully neglect their duties in that walk of life to which their bothers and sister-in-law have seen fit to call them.

Of course, when an aunt marries, she loses at once all the perfecting of the properly constituted aunt; and that is a thing to be seriously considered. Is she wise in leaving a profession for which all her sisters-in-law think she is admirably fitted, for one which the most experienced pronounce a lottery?

This is all of course written from Zerlina's point of view. She requires of a professional aunt many things. She must, to begin with, remember the birthdays of all her nephews and nieces, of Zerlina's children in particular. If she remembers their birthdays, it stand to reason, Zerlina's reason, that the sequence of thought is—presents.

The really successful aunt knows the particular taste of each nephew and niece. She knows, moreover, the exact moment at which the taste changes from a love for woolly rabbits to a passion for steam engines. Instinct tells her at what age a child maybe promoted, with safety, from wool to paint, and she knows the critical moment in a boy's life when a Bible should be bestowed. It usually, or perhaps I should say my experience is that it usually, follows the first knife, an ordinary two-bladed knife, and comes the birthday before a knife—with things in it." The real boy must have a knife with things in it: a corkscrew,—I wonder why a corkscrew?—a buttonhook, a thing to take stones out of horses' hoofs, a thing to mend traces with—I know I am ignorant of the technical terms—but the hardest-hearted shop-assistant will never fail to help a professional aunt in the choice of a knife, unless by chance he should be unhappy enough never to have been a boy, and such cases are rare.

I used often to wonder why boys wanted all these things. Now I know, bemuse I asked Dick and he said, You see, Aunt Woggles, I use them for other things." I am not sure that most of us don't do the same thing with many of our most cherished possessions in life.

As regards steam-engines Zerlina lays down a distinct law. They must never burst-that is an injury no sister-in-law would

Mary C.E. Wemyss

ever forgive—and paint must never come off. If Zerlina had known and loved the taste of crimson lake in the days of her youth, she would never draw so hard and fast a line.

From the earliest moment in a baby's career, the professional aunt takes upon herself serious responsibilities. She may not, for instance, like any ordinary aunt, pass the baby in his perambulator, out walking. Any other aunt may, with perfect propriety, say, "Hullo, duckie, where's auntie?" and pass on. She knows the danger of stopping, and seeks to avoid it. Not so the professional aunt. She realizes the danger and faces it. She knows she will have to wait, for the sake of the child's character, until he shall choose to say, "Ta-ta."

He will probably, if he is a healthy child, say everything he knows but that. He will go through his limited vocabulary in a pathetically obliging manner, making the most beautiful "moo-moos" and "quack-quacks," but he will not say, "Ta-ta." Why should he? On persuasion, and more especially if the interview should take place at a street-corner on a windy March day, he will repeat the "moo-moos" and "quack-quacks" even more successfully than before, and he will wonder in what way they fall short of perfection, since he earns no praise. He likes to be rewarded with, "Kevver boy." We all do, just as a matter of form, if nothing else. Surely ordinary politeness demands it.

He will not say, "Ta-ta," though. Who knows but what it is innate politeness on his part and his way of saying, "Oh, don't go! What a flying visit!"

However, the professional aunt cannot be sure of this, although she can guess; so she must wait patiently, for the sake of Baby's morals and nurse's feelings, until he does say, "Ta-ta." We may suppose that he at last loses his temper and says it, meaning, no doubt, "For goodness sake, go!" if not something stronger. The nurse is satisfied, the aunt is released, and the conscientious objector is wheeled away.

Besides ministering to the soul of a baby the aunt must tend to its bodily needs, and for this reason she must be a good needlewoman.

Before the arrival of the first nephew or niece, when she is very unprofessional, she will hastily put her work under the sofa or behind the cushion when any one comes into the room. As she grows older and more professional, and the nephews and nieces become more numerous, she will give up hiding her work. People who are intimately connected with the family will show no surprise, and to inquisitive strangers, unless she is very religious, she can murmur something about a crèche, so long, of course, as Zerlina is not there.

The really successful aunt, one who is at the top of her profession, can perfectly well be trusted to take all the children to the Zoo alone; that is to say, without a nurse, and of course without the mother. The mother knows how pleased and gratified an aunt feels on being given the entire charge of the children. The nurse is gratified too; in fact every one is pleased, with perhaps the exception of the aunt. But it is against professional etiquette for her to say so. She only wonders why mothers think a privilege they hold so lightly—taking the children to the Zoo—should be so esteemed by other women. But as the old story goes, "Hush, darling, hush, the doctor knows best," so must we say,—Mothers know best."

Another qualification in a professional aunt, desirable if not indispensable, is tact. If she should be possessed of ever so little, it will save her a considerable amount of bother. She won't, in a moment of mental aberration, praise dark-eyed children to Zerlina, whose children have blue eyes. Should she do so, by some unlucky chance, it would take several expeditions to the Zoo, and probably one to Kew, before things were as they were. If Zerlina, however, should, by the expedition of the aunt and children to Kew, be enabled to do something she very much wanted to do, and couldn't, because the nurse's father was ill, and the nursery-maid anemic, the little misunderstanding will have disappeared by the time the aunt returns from Kew, and Zerlina will say, after carefully counting the children,—it is this mathematical tendency in mothers that hurts an aunt,—"I do trust you implicitly with the children, dear. You know that; it isn't every one I could trust; you are so capable! I wish I were, but one can't be everything. Of course you don't understand a mother's feelings."

I sometimes wonder why Zerlina always says this to me. I have never pretended to be anything but an aunt.

But to return to my profession. As the children grow older the duties of the aunt become more arduous. For the benefit of schoolboy nephews with exeats, she must have an intimate acquaintance with the Hippodrome, any exhibition going, every place of instruction, of a kind, or amusement. She must be thoroughly up in matinees,, and know what plays are frightfully exciting, and she must have a nice taste in sweets. She need not necessarily eat them; it is perhaps better if she does not. But she must know where the very best are to be procured. She must never get tired. She must love driving in hansoms and going on the top of 'buses. She must know where the white ones go, and where the red ones don't, although a mistake on her part is readily forgiven, if it prolongs the drive without curtailing a performance of any kind. This requires great experience. She must set aside, moreover, a goodly sum every year for professional expenses.

The foregoing are a few of the qualifications which Zerlina thinks essential in aunts. There are others, and the greatest of them is love. Zerlina forgot to mention that.

CHAPTER II

But Diana! That is another story. Open the windows wide, let in the fresh air, the whispering of trees, the song of the birds, and all that is good and beautiful in nature. The very thought of Diana is sunshine. She is as God meant us to be, happy and good, believing in the goodness of others, slow to find evil in them, quick to forgive it, infinitely pitiful of the sorrows of the suffering. This is Diana, and she has three children, Betty, Hugh, and Sara. Allah be praised!

You do not imagine that I dislike Zerlina, do you? I should be sorry to give that impression. But a professional aunt must be above all things absolutely straightforward and truthful.

I had been engaged for weeks to go to Hames for the first shoot, and an urgent telegram from Zerlina, followed by a feverish letter, failed to move me from my purpose. The telegram, by the way, ran as follows: "Can you Tuesday for fortnight. Do. Urgent. ZERLINA." I wondered why Zerlina elected to leave out "come." If I had been strictly economizing, I should have saved on the "do." The letter followed in due course of time: -

> Dear Betty, I have just sent a wire in frantic haste asking you to come [that was exactly what she had not done] on Tuesday for a fortnight. I should so much like you to see something of the children, and Baby really is very fascinating. She is such a fat child, much fatter than Muriel's baby, who is six months older. The fact is, Jim is

rather run down; nothing much, of course, but I think a change would do him good, and the Staveleys have asked us to go to them, and I don't like to refuse, and we thought it would be such a good opportunity to have my bedroom re-papered and painted. I don't believe you would smell the paint, and in any case I believe there is some new kind of paint which smells delicious, like stephanotis, I am told, so I will order that. I would not ask you to come just as we are going away, because I should like to be at home to see you, but I could go away so happily if you were with the children; I often think for a woman without children, you are so wonderfully understanding, about children, I mean. You could manage nurse, too, I am sure. She is in one of her moods just now, and I feel I must get away from all worries for a little.

Yours,

ZERLINA

P. S.—Jim is so well, and would send his love if he were here.

I telegraphed back, of course, directly I got Zerlina's telegram, saying I could not come, and answered the letter at leisure. It is as a sister-in-law in relation to the aunt that Diana particularly shines. This aunt she looks upon as something more than useful, and asks her to stay at other times than when the children have measles, and whooping-cough, or the bedroom is to be re-papered. Zerlina perhaps is unfortunate. She says, "Have you ever noticed how the children always have something when you come to stay?" Zerlina is quite pretty when she puts her head on one side. I answer, "Yes, Zerlina, I have noticed it curiously enough," but I do not say that I suspect that at the very first sound of a cough, at the very first appearance of a rash, this aunt is urged to come and stay.

Diana accepts such services; the mother of such creatures as Betty, Hugh, and Sara is forced to do so by very reason of their existence. But those services she accepts with generous appreciation; not that an aunt wants thanks, but being human, pitifully so, even the most professional of them, she is conscious where they are not expressed, in some form or other. A smile is enough.

So to Hames I went, in spite of Zerlina's appeal, with treasures deep down in my box for Betty, Hugh, and Sara. Sara is of all babes in the world the most fascinating, say sisters-in-law other than Diana what they will. As a tribute to this fascination, the largest white rabbit, woolly to a degree undreamed of—at least I hoped so—in Sara's world, was carefully packed in my box, wrapped cunningly in tissue-paper, and guarded on all sides by clothing of a soft description. I have known a chiffon skirt put to strange uses in the interests of Sara.

I found the carriage waiting for me, and was touched to see that Croft, the old coachman, had come to meet me himself. It is an honor he does the family with perhaps two or three exceptions. When he comes to meet me,, there is a regular program to be gone through. It varies only in a very slight degree and begins like this: —

I say, "Well, Croft, it is very nice to see you," and he says, "The same to you, miss, and many of them." He then begins to "riminize"; the word is his own. He begins with the auspicious day on which I was born, and describes how he himself went to fetch the doctor in the dead of the night. He describes minutely his costume and the part the elements played on the occasion; they were evidently very much upset. He then goes on to say how h eheld me on my first pony, and taught me to ride and drive. Having finally certificated me as competent to drive a pair of horses under any circumstances, I ask how the children are, Sara in particular. Here Croft looks heavenward, and says she looks a picture, and adds that she looks very like me. The footman knows that here the program is at an end, Croft having no greater praise to bestow on mortal woman, and he opens the carriage door and I get in.

Diana knows what it is to travel t he distance of three miles in the suffocating embraces of Hugh and Betty; otherwise she would probably have sent the children to meet me.

The smell of the brougham brought my childhood vividly back to me. I shut my eyes and instinctively put out my hand; and that hand that was always held out to us as children took mine in its loving clasp, and I was a child again, home from a visit, so glad to feel that hand again and to see that mother from whom it was agony to be parted, for even a short space of time.

CHAPTER III

When I arrived at Hames, Diana, tall, fair, and beautiful as a Diana should be, was on the doorstep to meet me. Diana, by the way, had been christened "Diana Elizabeth," in case she should have turned out short and dumpy and, by some miraculous chance, dark. I looked for Sara in the tail of Diana's gown,—I am afraid this is a literary license, as Diana does not wear tails to her gowns in the country as a rule,—but Sara was not there.

"She is not there, said Diana. "The children are in the wildest state of excitement, and will you faithfully promise to go up and see them directly you have had tea?"

I would willingly have gone then and there, and murmured something about my box, and Diana said she hoped I had not brought them anything.

"Oh! nothing," I said; "only the smallest things possible"; knowing all the time that the woolly rabbit was, of its kind, unrivaled. But these are professional expenses, and what I spend does not afterwards give me a moment's worry. I have seen David, on the other hand, speechlessly miserable after buying a mezzotint, for the time being only, of course; the joy cometh in the morning, when Diana proves to him that it was the only thing to do, and that it was really quite wonderful, the way in which he was led to buy it. He had had no idea of doing so. Not the slightest! And yet something within him urged him to buy it. Absolutely urged him!

Mary C.E. Wemyss

Then, Diana said, it was clearly meant. If a man deliberately set out on a fine morning, bent on spending more than he could afford, then —! Diana's "then" is always so comforting.

I am so afraid you will spoil the children, she said; "they expect presents, which is so dreadful. Hugh bet sixpence at lunch that you would bring him something, and he said to poor Mr. Hardy, You didn't."

"But he will next time, Diana," I said.

"Of course he will; that is the dreadful part of it."

It is right that Diana should feel like that. A mother's point of view and another's, an aunt's, for instance, are totally different things, and I told Diana that, while fully appreciating her anxieties regarding the characters of her children, considered that to destroy a child's faith in an aunt was little short of criminal. But I promised that the next time I came I would, perhaps, not bring them anything. "But I shall give them fair warning."

Diana admitted the justice of this, and she said, with a sigh of relief, "I can't bear the children to be disappointed; a disappointed Sara is —"

"Diana," I interrupted, "is it wise to begin Saraing at this time of day?"

In reality the woolly rabbit was tugging at my heartstrings and clamoring to be unpacked. After a hurried tea, which I was obliged to have for the sake of Bindon's feelings, I went up-stairs, resolved to disinter at all costs, without delay, the rabbit. I felt great anxiety lest in transit the machinery which made the rabbit squeak in a way that surely no rabbit, mechanical or otherwise,—particularly the otherwise, I hoped,—had ever squeaked before, might be impaired; happily it was not.

Having carefully shut the door and silenced the attendant

housemaid, I took the precaution of burying the rabbit partially under the eider-down quilt before testing the squeak, so that no noise should reach the children. I am afraid I "mothered" the squeak of that rabbit if I imagined it could reach anywhere so far; it was in reality such a very small one. But such as it was, it was perfect, in spite of the deadening effect of the quilt, and I pictured Sara's dimples dimpling. How she would love it! The treasure was carefully wrapped up again, and I tried hard to make it look like anything rather than a rabbit, in case Sara should try, by feeling it, to discover its nature.

Jane, the housemaid, said that no one could tell, no matter how much they tried; if they tried all day, they wouldn't, that she knew for sure; which was very consoling.

I then examined Hugh's train and Betty's cooking-stove, and found them intact, with, the exception of a saucepan lid. This, after a search, we found under the wardrobe. Why do things always go under things? Jane didn't know—she only knew they did. Then I opened the door and called.

Suddenly I heard a noise unearthly in its shrillness: it was Hugh calling his Aunt Woggles. He threw himself into my arms, keeping one eye, I could not help noticing, on the parcels. During the hug, which gave him plenty of time to make up his mind, he evidently decided which was for him; for he relaxed his hold and went to the table by the window, on which the parcels lay, whistling in as careless a manner as a boy bursting with excitement could do. First of all he stood on one leg, then on the other, and looked knowingly at me out of the corner of his eye. He was too honest to pretend that he thought the parcel was for some other boy, since there was no other. When the excitement became more than he could bear, he sang in a sing-song voice, "I see it, I see it!"

"Open it, then," I said, which he proceeded to do with great energy, if with little success.

"I b'lieve it's a knife with things in it," he said.

My heart sank. "Oh, it's much too big for a knife, Hugh," I replied.

"I 'spect it is, all the same," he said with a nod; "you've made it big on purpose; I positively know you have."

At last it was opened, and I said, aunt-like, "Do you like it, Hugh?"

"Awfully, thanks." Then he added a little wistfully, "Tommy's got a knife with things in it, a button'ook."

Perhaps he saw I looked disappointed, for he added magnanimously, "I like trains next best, Aunt Woggles; only you see I didn't exactly pray for a train, that's why. What's Betty's?"

"Betty must open it herself."

"Don't you suppose," he said, "that she would like me to open it for her, because it is a hard thing opening parcels—and Betty says I may always open all her parcels when she is out."

"Hugh!" I exclaimed.

He rushed to the door. "Come on, Betty," he shouted. "Aunt Woggles wants you."

If Betty's entrance was less tempestuous than Hugh's, her embrace was not less ecstatic. She put her arms round my neck and took her legs off the ground,—a quite simple process, and known to most aunts, I expect. The ultimate result would, no doubt, be strangulation. No one knows, of course, but among aunts it is a very general belief. Unlike Hugh, Betty kept her eyes religiously away from parcels, and she got very pink when I drew her attention to the very nobly one which was hers. Hugh stood by, urging her to open it, and offering to help her;

but this Betty would not allow, and she opened it, her lips trembling with excitement.

"Is it for my very own?" she whispered.

"Absolutely for your very own, Betty," I answered.

"Oh!" said Betty. "Hugh, it's all for my very, very own; Aunt Woggles says so; but you may play with it when you are very good."

This in Hugh's eyes seemed so remote a contingency as to be scarcely worth consideration.

When the cooking-stove stood revealed in all its glory, Betty was silent for a moment; then she said in a voice choked with emotion, "I shall cook dinners for you, all for your very own self—nobody else."

My heart sank. "You will eat the things, won't you?" she asked, "if I make proper things, just like real things?"

"Of course," I said. "Where's Sara?"

"She wouldn't have her face washed," said Betty, "so she's waiting till she's good."

Poor Sara! A strict disciplinarian is Betty!

The regeneration of Sara was evidently a matter of moments only, for the words were hardly out of Betty's mouth when Sara, in all her clean, delicious dumpiness, appeared in the doorway. If there is one thing more delicious than a grubby Sara, it is a clean Sara. Sara after gardening is delicious, but Sara clean is assuredly the cleanest thing on God's earth. I have never seen a child look so new, and so straight out of tissue-paper, as Sara can look. She stared solemnly at her Aunt Woggles, and then proceeded to walk away in the opposite direction, which was an invitation on her part to me to follow and snatch her up in my arms. She bore the hug stoically for a reasonable time, and then said, "Oo 'urt."

I realized, with the agony of remorse, that a very large aunt can by means of a brooch inflict exquisite torture on a very small niece.

She wriggled herself free and began to rearrange her ruffled garments. "Yaya's got noo soos," she announced; "ved vuns."

"No, blue, darling," I said.

"Ved," said Sara.

"No, sweetest, blue," I repeated in a somewhat professional but wholly affectionate manner.

"Ved," said Sara with great decision; so I gave it up.

"Sara always thinks blue is red," said Betty; "don't you, darling?"

"No, boo," replied Sara; so the matter dropped.

"Oo's tummin' to see Yaya's toys," said Sara.

"Am I, darling? When?"

"Now."

"But Aunt Woggles has got something for you," I said in a triumphant voice.

Sara showed no interest and pulled me by the hand toward the door.

"Hand me that, Betty," I said, pointing to the parcel on the table.

Betty handed it to me.

"Here, Sara, I said, "I have got a darling white rabbit for you! Sara! A bunny!"

"Yaya's got a blush upstairs, a lubbly blush," she said, disdaining even to look at the parcel. I held it toward her, undid it, I squeaked the squeak, I called the rabbit endearing names; but to no purpose. Sara looked the other way. A look I at last persuaded her to bestow upon the rabbit; but she gazed at its charms, unmoved.

"Yaya doesn't yike nasty bunnies, only nice blushes," she said.

"It's a hearth-brush dressed up," whispered Betty, "and it's dressed up in my dolly's cape, at least in one of my dolly's capes; she loves it. Aunt Woggles, do you think it is a good thing to make hearth-brushes say their prayers? Sara does."

I followed Sara disconsolately to the nursery and was shown the beauties of the "lubbly blush."

Nannie bemoaned her darling's taste, and the nursery-maid blushed for very shame.

"Not but what it's quite clean, miss," Nannie said; "it's been thoroughly washed in carbolic."

Meanwhile Sara was rocking herself backward and forward in a manner truly maternal and singing her version of "Jesus Tender" to her "lubbly blush."

"I thought she would love the rabbit," I said, and Nannie, by way of consolation, assured me that there was really nothing Sara loved so much as a rabbit. I suppose Nannie knew, and that it was only another instance of the folly of judging from appearances.

"You will love your bunny, won't you, darling?" said Nannie;

"nice bunny! "

"Nasty bunny," said Sara with great decision.

"That's naughty, baby," said Nannie; "nice bunny!"

"Naughty bunny," said Sara, "vake Yaya's yubbly vitty blush." And she resumed her singing with religious fervor.

Nannie was really quite upset, and apologized for her charge. I accepted the apology and resolved then and there to send the despised rabbit to the Children's Hospital by the next post. Have you ever given a toy-balloon to a child, and had the child say, "Balloons don't amuse?" I have.

Nannie then, by way of consolation, suggested that Sara should say her prayers at my knee. It was the greatest compliment she could pay any one. Sara consented after much pressure, and she knelt down and proceeded to pack up her face. No other word to my mind describes the process. First of all she shut her eyes tight. To keep them tight seemed to require a great physical effort; this was done by tightly screwing up her nose. Next she proceeded to gather her eyebrows into the smallest possible compass, and then she drew a deep breath, folded her small hands, and started off at a terrific pace, "Gaw bess parver yan muvver yan nannie yan hughyan betty yan dicky an aunt woggles yan ellen yan emma yan croft—yan blusby yan all ve vitty children yan make dem velly good boys yan make my nastyole bunnyagoodgirl. May Yaya get up?"

"Not yet, baby, think," said Nannie.

Sara thought, and then with a fresh access of solemnity repeated an entirely new version of the Lord's Prayer. Nannie understood it evidently, for at a point quite unintelligible to me, Nannie said, "Good girl!" and Sara jumped up.

Nannie told me that nothing would induce Sara to pray that

she might be made good. She was always very ready to make such petitions on the behalf of Betty and Hugh, but for herself, no. She is not like Betty, who at her age prayed, "Dear God, please make me a good little girl, but if you can't manage it, don't bother about it; Nannie will soon do it."

Difficult and tedious as the task may have appeared to Betty, I think it was assuredly within the power of God to make her good without the intervention of Nannie. Dear Betty!

Sara was then put to bed, and while Nannie brushed her hair, Sara brushed the hearth-brush's hair. Sara was very anxious to have it in her bath with her, but here Nannie was firm.

Later the hearth-brush was dressed in a nightgown and laid beside Sara in her little bed. The last thing she did before going to sleep was to gaze at her darling "blush" with rapture and say, "Nasty—'ollid—bunny!"

Her eyelashes fluttered and then gently fell on her cheek, as a butterfly hovers and then settles on the petal of a rose.

"Leave it here, miss," said Nannie; "she'll see it when she wakes."

I left the despised bunny and went to dress for dinner. Betty was waiting for me outside. "Is the cooking-stove for my very own self, Aunt Woggles?"

"Absolutely, Betty. Why?"

"Only because Hugh wondered if it wasn't or him, too. He only wondered, and I said I didn't suppose one present could be for two people, because then it wouldn't be such a very real present, would it?"

I said, "Of course not"; and I told her the story of the two men who owned one elephant, and one man said to the other: "I don't know what you are going to do with your half; I am going to shoot mine!"

"And did he, Aunt Woggles? " asked Betty, her eyes wide with horror.

"I wonder," I said. "I'll race you to the end of the passage."

"I won," cried Betty. "No, we both of us did," she added, slipping her hand into mine.

That evening Diana told me that a few days before, she had heard the following conversation between Hugh and Betty:

"I am going to shoot my cock."

"Hugh!" said Betty, "don't, it's a darlin' cock."

"But it doesn't lay eggs," said Hugh.

"I don't think cocks are supposed to lay eggs," said Betty thoughtfully.

"Well, I don't see why they shouldn't," said Hugh; "widowers have children."

CHAPTER IV

Suppose all aunts, that is to say, all professional aunt, know what it is to be visited at seven o'clock in the morning by nephews and nieces, fresh, vigorous, and rosy after a night's rest. Fresh, and oh! so vigorous and deliciously rosy were Hugh and Betty when they appeared at my bedside at seven o'clock the next morning.

"Hullo!" said Hugh, "we've come. May we get into your bed? I'll get up steam and take a long run and jump in. Shall I?"

I braced myself up for the shock. There is no need to go through the morning's program; I suppose every aunt knows it. Bears, camel-rides, robbers, and various other things, all of a distinctly energetic nature. At half past seven-you see it doesn't take long, any aunt can bear half an hour—Nannie appeared, carrying a deliciously rosy Sara with her hair done on the top, which makes her more than ever fascinating; and in her arms she carried her bunny—Sara's arms, I mean, of course. "Nice bunny," she said.

"Who gave you your bunny?" I asked.

"Jesus!" said Sara, triumphantly nodding her head and opening her eyes very wide. "Jesus makes all ve bunnies, and all ve vitty dickey birds, and all ve vitty fowers, and all ve big fowers and all ve ponge cakes, and Yaya."

"And what is Sara going to do with her bunny?" I asked.

Mary C.E. Wemyss

"Vuv it," she said with ecstasy.

"Shall I leave her?" asked Nannie.

"What a foolish question, Nannie!" I said. "Could any one send away a blue dressing-be-gowned Sara?"

"And shall I take the others, miss?"

"Do," I replied.

They went and left me in sole possession of Sara.

"Shall I tell Sara a story?" I said. She nodded her head.

"A storlie all about bunnies."

So I began, "Once upon a time there was a big bunny."

"A vitty bunny," said Sara.

"A little bunny," I said. "Once upon a time there was a little bunny."

"A velly, velly vitty bunny," said Sara.

"Once upon a time there was a very, very little bunny, "I repeated, emphasizing the very, very little," as Sara had done. She cuddled into the bedclothes, evidently quite satisfied with the beginning as it now stood. "And the very, very little bunny lived in a nice hole—"

"A nice bed," said Sara, "a velly nice bed and not in a vitty bed, but in a velly big bed, a velly, velly big bed with Aunt Woggles."

"In a nice big bed with Aunt Woggles," I said, "and he was a very good little bunny."

At this Sara rose in the bed and looked at me very severely.

" Did he say his palayers eberly day?" she asked.

"No, not prayers, darling. Bunnies don't say prayers; children say prayers."

"Naughty bunnies!" said Sara with great severity.

Dreading a religious discussion, which Sara loves, I proposed changing the story to "The Three Bears." She acquiesced with jumps of joy up and down, just where one would not choose to be jumped upon, and said, "Ve felee belairs."

Here I fared no better: my version of the story was so hopelssly wrong, and I received such crushing correction at the hands of Sara, that I was glad to relinquish my office of story-teller and suggested that she should tell a story instead.

This was evidently what she had wanted to do all along, for she began at once. She tells a story very much as she says her prayers, at the same terrific pace certainly. First of all she swallowed and took a deep breath, then she began, "Vunce there was a vitty blush—and not a bad nasty blush—it said its palayers ebery morning an nannie said good girly an then the blush vent to sleep in a vitty bed with Yaya."

"Go slower, darling," I said. "Aunt Woggles can't quite understand."

"Yan—ven—Yaya—voke up ve vitty—belush said, 'Good-morning,' yan Yaya said, 'Good-morning,' yan it was a nice bunny yan not a nasty bunny any more."

Here Sara's thoughts were distracted, and the story ended abruptly for want of breath, or possibly of story. She refused to go on, and when pressed said with great decision, "Dey's all dead."

She then had her share of camel-rides and bears, and by the time Nannie came I began to feel that I had earned my breakfast. I was one of the first down, and Bindon was evidently waiting for me, because as I went into the dining-room he took up his position behind a certain chair, which action on his part plainly indicated that I was to sit there. I wondered why. Could it be that I had arrived at the age when it is advisable for a woman to sit back to the light at breakfast? Was this only another instance of Bindon's devotion to us all? That the credit of the family is paramount in his mind, I know! All this flashed through my mind, but I saw a moment later that it was not of my complexion that Bindon thought, for on a plate before the chair behind which he stood, lay a small dark gray wad about the size of a five-shilling piece. I hesitated., and Bindon said in an undertone, "Miss Betty made it." Not a muscle of his face moved.

I sat down and gazed at the awful result of my present to Betty. The—what shall I call it?—was gray, as I said before; it had a crisscross pattern on it, deeply indented, and snugly sunk in the middle of it was a currant. I sighed. My duty as a professional aunt was clear: had I not in a moment of weakness said I would eat anything Betty made, provided it was a proper thing? Had I here a loophole of escape? No, it was certainly, according to Betty's lights, a most proper thing. But why does dough, in the hands of the cleanest child, become dark gray?

Bindon, having done his duty by Betty, and not being able on this occasion to do it by both of us, made no further explanation. Like the first step, it is no doubt the first bite that costs most dearly; and while I was pondering whether to take two bites or swallow it whole, Mr. Dudley came in and sat down opposite me. He is a young man who thinks that no woman he doesn't know can be worth knowing. When by force of circumstances he comes to know a fresh one, he always tells her he feels as if he had known her all her life, and talks of a previous existence, and so gets over a difficulty. I felt that it was a tribute to Diana that he treated me so kindly, and I earned his gratitude and commanded his respect by refusing food at his hands. I said I liked helping myself at breakfast. He insisted, however, on passing me the toast. This I felt was apart from Diana altogether.

After a few moments the little gray wad attracted his attention, and his eyebrows expressed a wish to know what it was.

"Betty made it," I said.

"And what is it? "

"I wonder!" I said. "I think it must come under the head of black bread."

" What are you going to do with it?" he asked.

I answered, "Why, eat it, of course; only I can't make up my mind how. What should you say, two bites or a swallow?"

His interest was now thoroughly aroused; he had evidently never before met an aunt professionally. He looked at me solemnly and said, "You are going to eat that?"

"I am an aunt, you see," said; "a professional aunt."

"A what?" he asked.

"A professional aunt," I answered. "You are an uncle, I suppose."

"I am constantly getting wires to that effect, but I am hanged if I have ever eaten mud-pies."

"No, that is part of the profession," I said; "you see, I promised Betty."

Mr. Dudley relapsed into silence. I had given him food for reflection.

Mary C.E. Wemyss

Here Betty appeared, "not to eat anything," she carefully explained. Hugh came next, followed a moment later by Sara, who was beside herself with excitement, which was centered in the blue ribbon in her hair, to which she had that morning been promoted. A red curl had become more rebellious than its fellows, and it was tied up with a blue ribbon, in the fashion beloved of young mothers. Diana dislikes any reference made to poodles.

"Yaya's got a ved vimvirn in her har," she announced.

We all expressed the keenest interest and unbounded surprise. One very well-meaning person put down his knife and fork and said he was too surprised to eat any more breakfast; whereupon Hugh said, "You needn't be so very funny, because Sara doesn't understand those sort of jokes."

Whether Sara understood it or not, it seemed to encourage her to further revelations, and she announced with bated breath, "Yaya's got ved vimvims in her—"She opened her eyes very wide and nodded very mysteriously, and was about to suit her actions to her words and disclose the ribbons in question, when Diana, with a promptitude quite splendid, administered a banana. Sara ate some with relish, paused, and said in a loud voice, subdued by banana, "jormalies." She was not going to be put off with a banana.

Betty was very much shocked, and with a face of virtuous indignation whispered in my ear, "Sara means-" I hastily stopped Betty because her whispers are louder than Sara's loudest conversation and very much more distinct. And after all there is everything in the way a word is pronounced. Without any context I think "jormalies" might pass anywhere as a perfectly right and proper word, to be used on any occasion.

Hugh, too, had something to say on the absorbing topic of ribbons, and on such a subject I thought he might safely be trusted. On what an unsafe foundation is built the faith of an aunt!

"Aunt Woggles," he said, "has got pink ribbons in her nightie; it's lovely, and she doesn't do her hair in funny little things like—"

Here David distracted Hugh's attention by telling him an absolute untruth concerning a fox to be seen out of the window. The first of April is the only day in the whole year on which the word "fox" won't take him flying to the window.

Betty, perhaps by way of changing the conversation, said, "You did eat my cake, didn't you, Aunt Woggles?"

"Of course I did, Betty."

"Don't you believe it," said Mr. Dudley.

"I always believe my Aunt Woggles," said Betty with infinite scorn. "Was it nice, Aunt Woggles?" Mercifully she didn't wait for an answer, but continued: " I lost the currant three times, but I found it all right. I thought I had trodden on it, but I hadn't, because I looked on the bottom of my shoe and it wasn't there. I did have lots of currants, only when I dropped them Mungo ate them all up, except this one. He didn't eat this one because I stopped him. I said, 'Drop it, Mungo!' and he did. It was a good thing he didn't eat it, wasn't it? I made lines across, did you see ? All across the cake! I made those with a hairpin. It was a good plan, wasn't it? "

Somehow or other my breakfast had fallen short of my expectations. But what I had lost in appetite I had perhaps gained in other ways, for I had until then undoubtedly existed in the mind of Mr. Dudley only under the shadow of Diana's charming personality. I now took my stand alone, as the Aunt Woggles who ate mud-pies, I am afraid; but still it is something to have a separate existence. Is it?

CHAPTER V

Diana's children are of a distinctly religious turn of mind. I think most children are, and what wonderful, curious thing their religion is! Looking back to my own childhood, I remember thinking, or rather knowing, that the Holy Ghost was a Shetland shawl. We called our shawls "comforters"; we wore them when we went to parties in the winter. I will not leave you comfortless," could mean nothing else. To complete the illusion, we had in the nursery a picture of the Pentecost, the Holy Ghost descending in the form of a cloudy substance, not unlike a Shetland shawl. I was so sure that I was right, that I never thought of asking any one. When I grew older and told my mother, she said, "But why didn't you ask me, darling?" forgetting that when a child knows a thing it never asks; when in doubt it will ask, but not when it knows. It is a difficult and dangerous thing to shake a child's belief, and a pity, too. For if we could all believe as simply as a child does, how different it would make life! If Diana has a fault, it is that she takes her children too seriously. She thinks it is wrong to tell them, "Children should be seen and not heard," simply because they have asked a question she can't answer. Aunts have been known to do it as a last resource, on occasions of great danger.

Hugh wants to know if God put in the quack before he made the duck. It is difficult, isn't it, to answer that sort of question?

On another occasion he asked Betty if God was alive. Betty, eager to instruct, said, "My dear Hugh, God is a Spirit."

"Then we can boil our milk on him." That was a poser for Betty.

Diana was at a loss, too, when Hugh announced his intention of going to Heaven. She asked him what he would do when he got there. I thought the question a little unwise at the time. "Oh!" said Hugh, "stroll round with Jesus, I suppose, and have a shot at the rabbits."

Diana's position was a difficult one. It was this: if she told Hugh there were no rabbits in Heaven, he wouldn't pray to go there; and if she said there was no shooting in Heaven, Hugh would know for certain that his father wouldn't want to go there, and it wouldn't do for Hugh to think his father didn't want to go to Heaven. It was a difficulty, but Hugh's Heaven was or is a very real and very happy place to him. It is strangely like Hames; and isn't the home of every happy child very near to Heaven? Surely it lies at its very gates, which we could see if it was not for the mountains which intervene, those beautiful snow mountains, which foolish grown-ups call clouds.

Diana has come triumphantly out of situations more difficult, and she will no doubt surmount those connected with the spiritual upbringing of Hugh, Betty, and Sara.

It is the custom of Diana to read the Bible every morning with her children, and they resent any deviation from custom.

After breakfast on the particular Sunday over which this shooting-party extended, Hugh marched through the hall, where most of us were assembled) with his Bible under his arm, followed by Betty, carrying a smaller Bible. Hugh's seemed particularly cumbersome. He cast a reproachful glance at his mother and her guests, and said to Betty, "I will teach you, darling."

Betty said, "Can you, Hugh?" and he said, "Rather!"

Into the drawing-room he stumped, followed by the impressed Betty.

"You may come, Aunt Woggles," he said, "if you don't talk."

I promised not to talk, and sat down to write letters.

Hugh sat down on the sofa and Betty plumped down beside him. She carefully arranged her muslin skirts over her long black-stockinged legs, and then told Hugh to begin.

"What's it going to be about?" she asked.

"All sorts of things," said Hugh grandly. "Perhaps about Adam and Eve, and Jonah and the whale, and Samson and Elijah. Do you know the diff'rence between Enoch and Elijah? That's the first thing."

"No, I don't," said Betty reluctantly.

"Well, darling, you must remember the diff'rence is that Enoch only walked with God, but the carriage was sent for Elijah!"

"Was it a carriage and pair, Hugh?"

"More, I expect."

"What next, Hugh?"

"We'll just look until we find something." And Hugh opened the Bible.

"It's upside down," whispered Betty.

Hugh assumed the expression my spaniel puts on when he meets a dog bigger than himself—an expression of extreme earnestness of purpose combined with a desire to look neither to the right nor to the left, but to get along as fast as he can.

Hugh assumed an immense dignity and looked straight in front of him, just to show Betty he was thinking and had not heard what she said, while he turned the Bible round.

"Go on, Hugh," said Betty humbly, feeling it was she who had made the mistake. How often do men make women feel this!

"Now, Betty," he said, "you must listen properly and not talk, because it's a proper lesson, just like mother gives us when visitors aren't here." A pause, then Hugh said in a very solemn voice, "You know, darling, Jesus would have been born in the manger, but the dog in the manger wouldn't let him!"

I stole out of the room.

"You don't disturb us, Aunt Woggles," called out Hugh; "you truthfully don't."

Hugh had evidently told all he knew, for in a few minutes he came out of the drawing-room and joined us in the hall. "We've done!" he exclaimed; "we've had our lesson all the same."

"I am sorry, Hugh," said Diana.

He slipped his hand in hers as a sign of forgiveness, and by way of making matters quite right, I said, "You know, Hugh, mothers must look after their guests. Their children are always with them, but friends only occasionally."

Why do aunts interfere? Retribution speedily follows.

"Visitors are mostly always here," said Hugh plaintively. "When you have children of your own, Aunt Woggles, then—"

"A fox, a fox, Hugh!" cried some one.

He rushed to the window.

"That's two foxes today that weren't there when I looked," said

Hugh; "I shan't look next time."

This was a desperate state of affairs; an attack might come at any time, and we should have exhausted our ammunition.

"The best thing," said Diana, "is for those who are going to church to get ready."

Betty and Hugh were of course going; Sara wanted to, but those in authority deemed it wiser that she should wait till she was older. This offended her very much, as did any reference to her age. But the decision was a wise one: she prayed too fervently, she sang too lustily, and she talked too audibly, to admit of reverent worship on the part of the younger members of the congregation, and of the older ones, too, I am afraid.

One memorable Sunday she did go to church, as a great treat; and when the hymn—"Peace, perfect peace" was given out, a beatific smile illumined her face, and with her hymn-book upside-down she was preparing to sing, when Diana said, —whispered rather—You don't know this, darling."

"Yes, I do, mummy, peace in the valley of Bong."

Betty walked to church with me. "Aunt Woggles," she said, "you know the gentleman in the Bible who lived inside the whale?"

"Yes, darling," I said, "I do remember." My heart sank at the difficulties presented by Jonah as gentleman.

"Well," she said, "what dye suppose he did without candles in the dark passages of the whale?"

Betty evidently pictured the dark passages of the whale to be what Haines used to be before electric light was installed. The whale, like a house, must be modernized to meet the requirements of the day. When Betty starts asking questions, she mercifully quickly follows one with another, and does not wait for answers. The interior economy of the whale suggested various trains of thought, and she went skipping along beside me, or rather in front of me, propounding the most astounding theories. I was quite glad when Mr. Dudley and Hugh caught us up.

"You did come along fast, old man," said Mr. Dudley.

"It wasn't me, it was you," panted Hugh. "It truthfully was, Aunt Woggles, and he wasn't going to church at all till I told him you were going. I'm awfully out of breath because he wanted to catch you up, so it wasn't me all the time."

I was sorry Hugh and Mr. Dudley had caught us up.

Mr. Dudley murmured something about "Young ruffian," and I felt it my duty as well as my pleasure to tell Hugh not to talk so much.

"I 'sect you want to sit next my Aunt Woggles, don't you?" said Hugh to Mr. Dudley; "but you can't, because I said, 'bags I sit next Aunt Woggles in church' before she came to stay, ever so long before, before two Christmases ago, I should think it was, or nearly before two Christmases ago!"

Betty's grasp on my hand tightened, and I returned it with a reassuring pressure, as much as to say, "There are two sides to every aunt in church, dear Betty; it is a comfort to know that."

"I may sit next you, mayn't I?"

"Yes, Betty," I said.

"You are very rosy, Aunt Woggles," said Hugh. "Do you love my Aunt Woggles?" he continued, dancing backward in front of Mr. Dudley.

"Of course he does," I said boldly, taking the bull by the horns. "Mr. Dudley loves even his enemies, especially on Sundays."

Hugh looked puzzled, and pondered. Before he had come to any definite conclusion as to how this affected Mr. Dudley's feelings towards me, we reached the lichgate, where we found the rest of the party awaiting us. We all separated: Diana took Betty, who gazed at me mournfully, but was too loyal to her mother to say anything; Hugh gave a series of triumphant jumps, which added pain to Betty's already disappointed expression.

In church I found myself allotted to what we call the overflow pew, which is at right angles to the family pews and in full view of them. It is the children's favorite pew only, I imagine, because they don't always sit there. Hugh sat very close to me, and kept on giving little wriggles and gazing up at me, then at Mr. Dudley, and snuggling closer to me as if to emphasize the superiority of his position over that of Mr. Dudley.

"Hugh," I whispered, "you must behave."

"He didn't sit next you, after all," he whispered.

I say whispered, but must explain that Hugh's whisper is a very far-reaching thing. He loves a victory. I hope that when he grows up he will be a generous victor. He says he is going to be a dangerous man; I can believe it.

Betty, the vanquished one, stared solemnly in front of her, not deigning to notice Hugh's triumph. What pleasure is there to children in sitting next to some particular person in church? I remember, as a child, it was a matter of earnest prayer during the week that on Sunday I might sit next, some particular person in church. "And, O Lord, if it be for my good, let me sit next the door." A child's religion is a very real thing to him, and not only a Saturday-to-Monday thing.

I looked at Betty's serious little face and wished that I could for one moment read her thoughts. Her eyes, such lovely eyes, were fixed on the preacher's face. What did his sermon convey to her? It was a particularly uninteresting one, I remember, an appeal on behalf of the curates' fund. Her eyes never left his face—such solemn, searching, truthful eyes. I think a child like Betty should not be allowed to go to church on such occasions, for what is the use of preaching against matrimony on the one hand, and that, I suppose, is what the moral of such a sermon should be,—and on the other hand holding up an incentive to matrimony in the very alluring shape of Betty? For, personally, I think Betty would be a very wonderful possession for any curate to have.

Hugh was growing restless and I was bearing the brunt of it. Nannie, feeling for me, leaned over from the back pew and said, "Don't rest your head on your Aunt Woggles."

"I came to church on purpose to rest my head on my Aunt Woggles's chest," said Hugh, again in what he calls a whisper. A moment later, he asked, "Is it done?"

It was, and he jumped up.

"May I sit next you next Sunday, Aunt Woggles?" he said, so soon as we got outside the church door.

"No, Hugh," I said.

"I bet I do, all the same," he said.

"Aunt Woggles," said Betty, as we walked home, "I collect for the prevention of children; do you suppose Mr. Dudley would give me a penny?"

"I am sure he would, darling, but it is the prevention of cruelty to children—the prevention of cruelty."

"That's such a long thing to say, Aunt Woggles, don't you suppose he would understand if I did say it a little wrong?"

"Perhaps, darling, but it is always best to say things right."

"Yes, I will, but I was only supposing, supposing I didn't."

At luncheon Diana cautioned Betty against swallowing a fish-bone. "You might die, darling, if you did."

"Then I shall swallow every single bone I can," announced Betty.

"But, darling," said Diana, "why do you say that? You don't want to die. You are quite happy, aren't you?"

"Yes, I'm very happy, but I want to die, all the same."

"Oh, darling, don't say that," said Diana; "there is a great deal for you to do in this world before you die."

"Yes, but you see, darling," said Betty, "if I don't die soon, I shall be too old to sit on Jesus' knee."

Diana is very particular about the children's manners, and Hugh came face to face with a great difficulty a moment later, over his ginger beer. "If I don't say I thank you, mother doesn't like it, and if I do say I thank you, Bindon stops pouring."

CHAPTER VI

In answer to a really desperate telegram from Zerlina, I left Hames hurriedly, and arrived at Zerlina's, to find her out and all the children apparently well. I was shown upstairs into the drawing-room. In Diana's house I am never "shown" anywhere; however, in Zerlina's I am, so it is no use discussing that question. The drawing-room into which I was shown was empty of furniture except for the sofas and chairs which were arranged round the room against the wall. As Zerlina's room does not err as a rule on the side of emptiness, I realized that there was going to be a party. I felt like the child who said, "There's been a wedding, I smell rice!" One knows these things by instinct.

The butler solemnly informed me that there was going to be a party, and that Miss Hyacinth would be down in a moment.

I thought it odd that Zerlina should have said nothing about a party; but then she never says anything about measles, or whooping-cough, or re-painting rooms, until I am within the doors and unable to escape. I remembered she had urged me on this occasion to come early. I sat down on a sofa and sadly fixed my gaze on the parquet floor. How different had been my arrival at Hames! My conscience smote me. I had no train, no cooking stove,, no woolly rabbit in my box. But then neither was there a Hugh, Betty, and Sara. At Hames should I have sat in the drawing-room? Never! Of course I know what some people will say: that it is my fault; if I had treated the children as I treated Betty, Hugh, and Sara, it would have

Mary C.E. Wemyss

made all the difference; but it wouldn't, really. It is, the mother of the children who makes the difference; it is her attitude to the aunt which is adopted by the children. If Diana had been out, the house would have resounded with shrieks for Aunt Woggles. But in Zerlina's house children never shriek, people never rush to the nursery. The children are always tidied before they are brought down to see me.

Of course some people will again say, "Quite right"; and it is quite right that for such people they should be tidied; but do those people realize what a wall tidiness builds between child and grown-up? Have they ever thought what a boy feels when his mother comes down to see him at school and the first thing she does when he comes into the room is to say that his collar is dirty, or that his hands want washing? At that moment, perhaps, she lays the first brick in the wall which builds between mother and son. He is a happy boy and she a blessed mother who stand always with no wall between them. All a boy demands of his mother when she comes to see him at school is that she shall behave just like other people, and that she shall dress properly. If she can be beautiful, so much the better: it will redound enormously to his credit. Boys are very sensitive about their belongings, but when praise can be bestowed they bestow it, as in the case of Tommy, who wrote to his father, who had been down to the school to play in a match, "Fathers against Sons, "Dear father, you did look odd, but you made the second biggest score."

While I was pondering over these things, the door opened and my niece Hyacinth came in.

"Hullo!" she said; "mum's out."

"So I hear," I said; "won't you kiss me?"

"Oh! I forgot," she said, twirling round on one leg and holding out a cheek to be kissed. "There's going to be a party to it."

"So I see, I said; "what sort of a party?"

"Oh! it's the end-up of the dancing class, four to seven; that's why mum asked you to come early."

"She isn't in yet?" I asked innocently.

"Oh! she's not coming," said Hyacinth, raising her eyebrows and laughing; "she always has something to do on dancing days. The Frauleins get on her nerves. They sit all round the room."

And Hyacinth indicated the position of the Frauleins with a sweep of her arm.

"What time is it now?" I asked.

"Half past three," she said; "I'm ready."

"I'm not," I said savagely.

I went upstairs, vowing vengeance on Zerlina. I could have shaken Hyacinth, poor child, and why? Because her legs were too long, or her skirts too short, or the bow in her hair too large? What a disagreeable, cross-grained professional aunt I was! Or did I miss the hug Hyacinth might have given me?

I was only just ready when the children began to arrive. I flew downstairs and found not only children in every shape and form, but mothers in big hats and trailing skirts, and Frauleins in small hats and skirts curtailed, mademoiselles and nannies. The nannies I handed over to the nursery department, and the mothers and the Frauleins and the mademoiselles I arranged in a dado round the room., making inappropriate remarks to each in turn. No surprise was expressed at the absence of Zerlina.

The children began to dance. There was a particularly pains-taking little boy in a white silk shirt and black velvet knicker-bockers, very tight in places, who danced assiduously, looking neither to the right nor to the left. "Right leg, To-mus, left leg,

To-mus!" came in stentorian tones from a Fraulein in the corner, who suited her actions to her words by the uplifting of the leg corresponding to that recommended to Tomus's consideration, and bringing it down with emphasis on the parquet floor.

By the sudden quickening of leg-action on the part of my painstaking friend, I knew him to be Tomus, and by that only, so many of the boys looked as if they might be Tomus. The real Tomus asserted himself manfully, however, by using the exactly opposite leg to that ordered by Fraulein. I liked this spirit of independence, and determined to make friends with him so soon as that dance should be over. I took the liberty of introducing myself; he made no remark but took me by the hand and led me out on to the landing, and there he found two chairs in the orthodox position. Into one of these he wriggled himself by a backward and upward movement, and I sat in the other. How absurdly easy it is for a grown-up to sit down! I waited for Thomas to make a remark; I might be waiting still, if I had not made a beginning. He looked at me under his eyelashes, and tried not to smile. It was an effort, I could see, and I could tell just where the dimples would come. When the effort became too great and the dimples asserted themselves beyond recall, he looked away and put out a minute portion of his tongue. Having done that, he subsided into grave self-possession.

I began to feel embarrassed, and asked him how old he was. He smiled. "Do you like dancing, Thomas?" I said.

He looked away, and every time I addressed him he seemed to retreat farther into his chair, until I had fears that he would disappear altogether from my sight. His waist-line seemed to be the vanishing-point. I made no further effort, and relapsed into silence. Thomas continued to gaze at me and smile. At last he extended a fat little hand, uncurled one by one four soft little fingers, and revealed, lying in his palm, a short screw. It was evidently his greatest treasure, for the moment.

"Is that for me, Thomas?" I asked. "Nope," he said, shaking his head.

"Is it your very own?"

"Yeth," said Thomas, drawing in his breath. He shut his little hand, put out his tongue just the smallest bit, and became serious and silent.

"Is it a present?" I asked. Having got so far, it seemed a pity not to go on. He had done me the greatest honor that a small boy can do a woman, which, by the way, was what our Nannie said when she told us that a strange man had proposed to her on a penny steamboat.

Thomas shook his head and said, "Nope."

"Did you find it?" I asked.

He nodded. "I always find fings," he said.

Beyond that I could get nothing out of him. I have not often sat out with a more embarrassing partner. To be continually stared at and never spoken to would, I think, make the boldest woman shy. There was a stolidity about Thomas that promised well for England's future. There was a steady resistance from attack that was really admirable; but I was not altogether sorry when Fraulein pounced upon him. As she led him off I heard him say, "Parties do last a long time, don't they, Leilein?"

Having lost Thomas, I sought a new partner. A tall, fair girl with wide, gray eyes, a pink-and-white complexion, a beautiful mouth, and a delicately refined nose, interested me, as I imagine she has continued to do every one who has met her. She reminded me of spring, with birds singing and flowers flowering and trees bursting, just as Diana does. As it was quite the correct thing for girls to dance with one another, I made so bold as to ask her for a dance. With the timidity of a boy just out of Etons, or perhaps I should say, of a shy boy just out of

Etons, I approached her. "Right-o," she said, "let's see."

She puckered her penciled eyebrows and studied her program. "The third after the two next?"

She bowed gravely, and I said, "Thank you." I felt very young and inexperienced as I returned the bow.

"That's all right," she said. "Where shall I find you? It doesn't matter, I shall know you again"; and she had the audacity to write on her program, for I saw her do it, "white dress, red hair."

She was borne off by a triumphant boy, who looked at me as much as to say, "You're jolly well sold if you think you are going to nab this dance."

I asked a hungry-looking boy with many freckles who she was. "Oh! that's Dolly," he said; "she is a flyer, isn't she?"

"Dolly who?" I asked.

"Oh! just Dolly; that does." He looked away, looked back, hesitated, and swallowed. I, feeling that he perhaps needed the assistance a man sometimes requires of a woman, encouragement, smiled at him.

"You wouldn't dance this, I suppose?" he said.

"Certainly," I answered.

We danced. He was a nice boy, very much in earnest, very much afraid of tiring me, very much afraid of letting me go, too shy to stop, until I suggested it, for which act of consideration he seemed grateful.

He told me he had five brothers, all older than himself; that he never had new trousers, always the other boys' cut down; that he liked school; wanted a bicycle more than anything in the world—of his very own, of course; wanted a pony of his very own; wanted a dog of his very own. He hadn't anything of his very own.

I said I supposed he thought his eldest brother very lucky.

"Because of the trousers?" he asked.

I said, "Well, yes, I suppose he has the new ones."

"Well," he said, "you see he doesn't. That's the chowse of the whole thing. He is the eldest, but you see Dick's the biggest, so he gets the new trousers. It is hard, isn't it?"

I said it was indeed.

"The best of it is," he said, "I am catching jackup. He is in an awful wax. I shouldn't be surprised if I were bigger than him next holidays. Do you like dancing? I simply loathe it—not with you, I don't mean I."

He told me many other confidences, and I was really sorry when he remembered, with an evident pang, that he had to dance with that "rum little kid over there."

I was quite certain that he would never break a promise. I could picture him going through life always keeping promises, rashly made, no doubt. I wondered what he would talk to girls about atdances years hence—trousers? Hardly. By that time he would have trousers of his very own, and they would cease, in consequence, to be things of interest.

He would be a soldier—of that I could have no doubt. He was the kind of boy England wants and can still get, thank God! say pessimists what they will.

While I was awaiting my Dolly dance, I came upon a small, disconsolate boy.

"I'm looking for an empty partner," he said.

I captured a passing girl, very small, and they danced away together. The boy I could see was very energetic, the girl was very small and fat. As they passed me I heard her say, "I—can't—go—so—fast!"

"Very sorry," said the small boy, "but I must keep up with the music."

Dolly found me. "I think I had better dance gentleman," she said; "I think I am as tall as you." With a tremendous effort she drew her slim figure to its full height, and, gazing up into my face she had the audacity to say, "Yes, I do just look down upon you; anyhow, men aren't always taller than girls. My cousin says so, and she goes to dances—heaps—and she is six foot."

We started off, I felt at once, on a perilous course. "You see," she said, "I had better—steer—because" (bump we went into somebody), "because—I dance once a week—always" (crash), "sometimes oftener—so I get—plenty of practice" (bang) "in steering, and that helps. I love dancing—don't you? Oh, that's all right—it's—only—the stupid—old mantelpiece—I always go into that—it sticks out so—doesn't it? It is hard—rather!"

Dolly was a flyer and no mistake. I was brought to a standstill at last by colliding with Thomas's Fraulein.

"It's all right," said Dolly generously, "you didn't hurt us!"

Fraulein was hurled on to a sofa and made no remark. She gave up temporarily the management of Thomas's left leg.

"Shall we sit out?" said Dolly. "It is hot, isn't it?"

She fanned herself with a very small program and tossed her hair back from her face. It was such lovely hair.

"Hair is beastly stuff, isn't it?" she said. "Wouldn't you love to be a boy? Oh, I promised mother not to say I 'beastly'; that's one of the things I would like to be a boy for, because boys may do such an awful lot of things."

I soon found out that Dolly liked boys better than girls.

She loved horses and dogs.

She hated and detested bearing-reins.

She didn't want to come out.

She thought grown-ups silly, except some -

She loved the country and strawberry ice.

She hated dull lessons, and I very soon discovered that there were none other than dull.

She collected stamps.

She longed to have a pet monkey or a brother, she didn't much mind which.

At the mention of brothers I looked down at Dolly's slim legs, clothed in fine black silk stockings, at the valenciennes lace on her muslin frock, and I imagined that if she had any brothers, the younger ones would be quite likely to have started life in trousers of their own. Yes, Dolly looked like it. I learned a great deal from her in the time it had taken me to get "yeth" and "nope" out of Thomas.

The energetic boy who had been obliged to keep up with the music at all costs, the little fat girl's in particular, came up to me, and said in an aggrieved voice, "Miss Daly has spoilt my program; she can't write, and she has written big D's all over it. Will you write me out a fresh one?"

Which I, of course, did. Really it was very careless of Miss Daly.

The children danced hard, with intervals for tea and refreshment; and as seven o'clock struck, there was a transformation scene. With conscientious punctuality the party-dressed children turned, into little or big woolen bundles, as the case might be. The last bundle I saw was a pink woolen one, weeping bitterly. My heart was wrung. The noisy crying of a child is bad enough, but when it is the soft weeping of a broken heart, it is unbearable. Of course it was my friend Thomas. I stood on the staircase unable to do anything, for he was quickly borne from the arms of Fraulein by a big footman, and no doubt deposited in a brougham in the outer darkness. Poor Thomas!

I hoped that the right sort of mother would be at home to unroll that pink bundle, a mother who would pretend that it could not be her darling who was crying, but a strange little boy with a face quite unknown to her. Where could he have come from? And so on, until Thomas would be ashamed to be seen with a strange face, and would smile, and then his mother would say, "What is it, my darling?" because, of course, it was her own darling who was crying, and she would never rest till she knew why.

I went back to the drawing-room quite happy that Thomas should be unrolled by the right sort of mother, and as I walked across the room, my foot slipped on something. I looked to see what it was I had trodden on. It was a short screw, Thomas's precious possession. "That was why the poor pink bundle was crying!"

"Hyacinth," I said, "who was Thomas?"

"Which one? There was little Thomas and the Thomas who lives a long way off, and then just plain Thomas."

"I mean the fat little Thomas who danced so hard."

"Oh! that's the little Thomas," said Hyacinth.

"Where does he live?" I asked.

"Oh, quite close; when we go to tea there we walk. He hasn't got a mother, so there's no drawing-room. She died," added Hyacinth, as if it was an every-day occurrence that Thomas should be left without a mother, instead of its being a heart-breaking tragedy. A child with no mother, no mother to unwrap the pink bundle, no mother to grieve for the screw, no mother to understand things. Perhaps his mother had been a Diana sort of mother.

"Oh, Thomas," I thought, "I must send you back your screw." I didn't care what any one said—he should have it.

If he had had a mother, it wouldn't have mattered, because she would have known it was a screw he had lost, and she would have known just what comfort he would have needed; whereas a Fraulein would know nothing about a screw, beyond the German for it, and the gender, of course. And of what use is that to a child? It may sound very unconventional, and I suppose it was so, to go to a strange house and ask for Thomas, and my only excuse a small screw. But still I went!

I pictured a lonely child in a large house with a Fraulein and a nurse, perhaps two; those I could face. A tall, sad father I had never thought of! I am afraid I am not suited for the profession, I am too impulsive.

I rang the bell. The door was opened by a solemn man-servant, who did not show the surprise he must have felt when I asked for Master Thomas. Another, still more solemn, showed me into a downstairs room. I refused to give my name, and a very large, serious Thomas rose from a chair as I was ushered in, "A lady to see Master Thomas." So my errand was in part explained, but the part left to tell was by far the most difficult. If only Thomas had lost anything but a screw! No father could be expected to know how it had been treasured. Supposing

Thomas had been crying because he had a pain, which sometimes comes to children after tea? Supposing he hadn't been crying for his screw at all? Supposing he repudiated all knowledge of it?

But here I was, screw in hand, and my story to tell. I told if. I was grateful to the tall, sad Thomas for being so solemn, and not even smiling, when I mentioned the screw. He said he was very grateful for my kindness, and he went so far as to say he was sure Thomas had valued the screw.

While some one was coming, for whom he had rung, he told me that when he had taken Thomas to the Zoo, the only thing which he was really excited about was the mouse in the elephant's house! Somehow or other that little story put me at my ease, for it showed that the big Thomas at least understood in part the mind of a child.

A nurse, not sad-looking I was glad to see, came in answer to the bell, and the big Thomas asked if the little Thomas had lost a screw? In that I was disappointed, the best nurse in the world might not know of a screw. But the big Thomas did not wait to hear; be was sure the little Thomas had, and he said we were coming upstairs to restore it to him. Of course I had said by this time that I was Zerlina's sister-in-law.

We went upstairs, I following the tall Thomas, past the drawing-room, past that bedroom whose door I knew was closed. A mother's bedroom is nearly always in the same place in a London house, a child blindfolded could find it, and the handle of a mother's door is always within the reach of the smallest child; and so easily does it turn, that the door opens at the slightest pressure of the smallest fingers.

Up we went to Thomas's own bedroom. There in his bed he sat, no longer crying, but still sad and solemn, with evidences in his face of a sorrow that rankled. He smiled when he saw me, too much of a gentleman to show any surprise at seeing me in his bedroom. "Thomas," I said, "I have brought you back your screw which you lost." I put it in his outstretched hand, and a smile rippled all over his face.

Suddenly from out the darkness came a stentorian voice, "Right hand, Tomus!" It was Fraulein! Thomas put out his right hand, and I, putting aside all convention, gave him a real "Sara hug" for the sake of that mother whose door was closed. It then began to dawn upon me how very unconventional it was of me to be hugging a comparatively strange child, in a perfectly strange house, and I hastily said good-night to the small Thomas and the big Thomas, nurses and Fraulein, and literally ran downstairs, followed of course by the big Thomas. At the foot of the stairs I ran into the arms of Mr. Dudley.

His exclamation of "Aunt Woggles" was involuntary, I felt sure, and he had every right to visit a sad, tall Mr. Thomas. But I thought Diana ought to have told me that I was likely to meet him at—Well, a stranger's house; so how could she? The only thing that consoled me was that in all probability Mr. Dudley would explain my profession in life, and that I had a screw loose. Yes, that would exactly explain the position. Otherwise I didn't exactly know how he could describe me.

Well, Zerlina of course said I was mad. She didn't agree with me that the screw could not possibly have been sent back in an envelope with a few words of explanation. She said she would have bought a nice toy for the child. What's the good of a toy to a child when he has lost a screw which he found his very own self, any more than a squeaking rabbit is to a child who has a "lubbly blush"? That was a lesson I had lately learned.

I didn't say all that to Zerlina, because, you see, she is a mother, and I couldn't understand these things. She was very much surprised at being late for the party, so surprised. She was full of apologies.

It was so good of me to help her! Had the darling children enjoyed themselves?

I said, yes, they had, and the adorable mothers, and the delicious Frauleins, and the heavenly mademoiselles. At this Zerlina looked a little pained, and I was sorry I was cross, but I felt her want of sympathy for Thomas. But then she had never passed that closed door.

CHAPTER VII

As a professional aunt must live somewhere, if only to simplify the delivery of telegrams, it is as well perhaps to explain where I live and why. The answer to the where, is London, and to the why, because it is the best place for all professionals to live in. Many were the suggestions that I should live in the country. Careful relatives and good housewives saw a chance of cheap and fresh eggs, cheap and large chickens, and cheap and freshly gathered vegetables, which showed, in the words of Dr. Johnson, a triumph of hope over experience, for I have always found that there are no eggs so dear as those laid by the hens of friends, no chickens so thin as those kept by relatives, no vegetables so expensive as those grown by acquaintances. But a professional aunt would of course be expected to make special terms, although her hens, like those of other people, would eat corn, and railways would charge just the same for carrying her goods, whether they were consigned to sisters-in-law or not, and the expense of the carriage is the reason invariably given why things are so dear when bought from friends. Friends, too, have a way of sending chickens with their feathers on, whereas the chickens one knows by sight, laid in rows in poulterers' shops, have no association with feathers. Don't you dislike the country friend who asks you to spend a night, and then tells you at breakfast that the pillow you slept on was filled with the feathers of departed hens known and loved by her?

Then there was Nannie, and my, living in London added a great importance to her position. She became at once chaperon, housekeeper, counselor, and friend. It was a great joy to

Mary C.E. Wemyss

her to think that she shielded me from the dangers of London; and she would willingly have fetched me from dinners and parties generally, and saw nothing incongruous in the announcement, " Miss Lisle's nurse is at the door."

"Not that I should be at the door," said Nannie; "I never go anywhere but what I am asked inside and treated as such." Nannie still thinks of us as children, and will continue to do so, no doubt until she who has rocked so many babies to sleep shall herself be enfolded in the arms of Mother Earth—and tenderly bidden to sleep.

Personally I had a leaning toward a flat, so many of my friends told me of the joys of shutting it up when one goes away, which, by the way, I find they never, or very rarely, do. But Nannie didn't hold with flats. It is curious what things people don't hold with. After reading of a terrible murder in a railway carriage, I cautioned my little housemaid, who was going home one Sunday, to be careful not to be thrown out of a window. She replied, "I don't hold with girls who are thrown out of windows."

Well, Nannie didn't hold with flats. To please me and to show her open-mindedness, she went with me to look at flats, but there was a tactless integrity about her criticism. I discovered that she judged of everything from a nursery point of view; and when I ventured to suggest that, as there were no children, a nursery was not of very great importance, she said, "You never can tell." In this instance I felt I could most distinctly tell, and wondered whether I might too tell Nannie of something I didn't hold with. But I didn't. I remember once long ago one of us asking Nannie if any one could have children without being married, and Nannie answered in a very matter of fact voice, "They can, dear, but it's better not." Anyhow, she didn't hold with flats. "There's the porters for one thing," she said. That, of course, settled it, and we looked at small houses.

"I suppose you will get married one of these days," she said, as we stood on a doorstep waiting to be let in.

"Perhaps no one will have me," I said.

"Well, they might; people marry you least expect to. Look at Maria Dewberry; you would never have—"

The door opened, or we will presume so, as my knowledge of Maria's movements after her surprising marriage is nil.

Looking over houses is not without excitement, and certainly not without surprises; but I was spared the experience some unknown person had who came one day to see our house when we all lived in London, but happened to be away. Having a house in the country, we very often did let the London house, which accounts for the agent's mistake.

One day, just as Archie was going out, he found on the doorstep a charming lady with a very pretty daughter.

"May we see over the house?" she asked.

"Certainly," said Archie.

He showed them all over the house, from cellar to garret. He says he initiated them into the mysteries of the dark cupboard, and he says he showed them everything of historic interest in the family. The daughter, he vows, was tremendously interested. When they had seen everything and Archie had brought them back to the hall, the charming mother said, "And when is the house to let?"

"Oh! it's not to let," said Archie.

He says he assured them it was no trouble at all, etc.!

In every small house we went, Nannie trudged laboriously up to the top, and I heard her murmuring, "Night, day," as she went backward and forward, from one room to the other. At last we found a small house in Chelsea of which she thoroughly approved. She couldn't exonerate the agent from all blame in saying that there were views of the river from the window. "Not but what there might be if we, leaned out far enough, but we can't because of the bars." It was the very bars that had attracted her in the first instance, from the outside. Bars meant a nursery. Iron bars may not make a cage, but they undoubtedly make a nursery.

She stood at the top window and looked out on the green trees, and a blackbird was obliging enough, at that very moment, to sing a love-song. Perhaps it was about nurseries, and Nannie understood it; at all events she decided there and then to take the house. " Of course, she said, "I know there's no nursery wanted, but I don't hold with houses that can't have nurseries in them, if they want to." That gave me an idea! It came like a flash. Nannie should have her nursery!

Of course this all happened some years ago, when the home at Hames was broken up. With the help of Diana I managed it beautifully. It was kept a dead secret. Diana collected, or rather allowed me to collect, all the things Nannie had specially loved in the home nursery, which I am sure cost Diana a pang, as she was very anxious her children should abide by tradition and grow up among the things their father had loved as a boy; but she sent them all, even the rocking-horse, to me for my nursery.

The walls I had papered just as our nursery had been papered. Even the old kettle was rescued from oblivion,, and stood on the hob. It was so old that any jumble sale would have been pleased to have it. The kettle-holder hung on the wall, with its cat on a green ground, which had been lovely in the day of its youth. One of us had worked it; Nannie of course knew which. The tea-set was there with its green, speckled ground.

But while all this was being arranged, Nannie had a very bad time. It was not for long, certainly, but she said it was pretty bad while it lasted. To insure the complete secrecy of our nursery plan, we arranged that she should go to Hames while we were doing it all, never thinking of what she would feel on going into the Hames nursery and finding all her treasures gone, and finding another woman reigning in her place; for all through our grown-up years the nursery had been left for Nannie as it had been when we were children. The nurse in her place hurt most.

"'Mrs.' here and 'Mrs.' there, certificated and teaching. It's all very well, but I'm not sure they don't go too far in this teaching business. No amount of teaching will—Well, it's there, so what's the use? I expect Eve knew how to handle Cain right enough."

"He wasn't very well brought up, though, Nannie," I said.

"Poor child! " said Nannie. " How do we know it wasn't Abel's fault? He may have been an aggravating child; some are born so, and I've seen a child, m any a time, go on at another till he's almost worried him into a frenzy just saying, 'I see you,' over and over again, does it sometimes. Children will do it, of course; besides, there were no commandments then, and you can't expect children to do right without rules and regulations. That's all discipline is, rules and regulations, which is commandments, so to speak."

"You think, then, Nannie," I said, "that Eve forgot to tell Cain not to kill Abel?"

"Well," said Nannie, "Eve had a lot to do; we can't blame her. She must have had a lot to do. Think what a worry Adam must have been: he had no experience, no nothing; he couldn't be a help to a woman., brought up as he was, always thinking of himself as first, as of course he was! Now, there's Parker—he is a good husband: he rolls the beef on Sunday to save Mrs. Parker trouble, and prepares the vegetables; he is a good husband, no trouble in the house whatsoever. He never brings in dirt, Mrs. Parker says, wipes his feet ever so before he comes, on the finest day just the same."

I thought the comparison a little hard on Adam, but still I

didn't say so, and Nannie reverted to the modern nurse, after informing me that men and horses were sacred beasts!

"Well, about nurses, 'Mrs.' before a nurse's name doesn't soothe a fretful child, nor make her more patient or loving. It might make her less patient, if she took to wishing the 'Mrs.' was real instead of sham; some women are like that, all for marrying. I dare say," said Nannie, when going over her experiences, "my face did look blank when I missed all my treasures, but f said nothing, although it was a blow when I thought of all the lovely times you had had with that rocking-horse. You remember the hole in it? Well, that was cut out solid because of all the things that were inside that rocking-horse; almost all the things that had been lost for years we found in that horse. My gold chain, for one thing, to say nothing of other things. The tail came out, and that is how the things got lost. The boys, always up to mischief, just popped anything they came across down that hole and put in the tail again, so no one knew anything about it. Well, then, your father lost something very special, I forget what, and there was a to-do! And Jane said she believed there was a power of things down that rocking-horse, so we got Jane's sister's young man, who was a carpenter, or by way of being, to come and cut out a square block out of the underneath—well, the stomach—of that horse—and then we found things! Things we had lost for years. Then we put the block back, and no one would have noticed particularly, not unless they had looked. Well, that's what I missed, the rocking-horse, but still I said nothing. Then we had tea out of new cups, and still I said nothing, because tea-cups will get broken, and you can't expect young girls to take care of cups like we did. The kettle-holder was gone! Then Mrs. David came in. Oh! she is lovely and like your mother in some ways, —the ways of going round and speaking to every one,—and she laid her hand on Betty's head, just as I've seen your mother do a hundred times on yours, and that was hard to bear. Anyhow, it's a good thing it wasn't some one else who got Hames. There 's that to be thankful for. It begins with 'Z,' you know."

"Nannie!" I said.

"Z for Zebra," said Nannie.

When the new nursery was all ready, Nannie was sent for. A dozen times that day I ran up that narrow staircase, and in the morning I laid the tea to see how it would look, and it looked so pretty that I left it. At four o'clock the fire was lighted and the kettle was put on to boil. Nannie drove up in a four wheeler. I was in the hall to meet her. She lingered to look at everything. She went round and round the dining-room, up to the drawing-room, even into the spare room, but no word of nursery. "Which is my room?" she said.

"It's upstairs," I said. "Won't you come and look at it?"

"There's no hurry, is there, miss?"

I could see it was the nursery floor she dreaded.

"Well, there is rather a hurry, Nannie," I said. "I am so anxious to see if you like all the house."

At last I got her upstairs. I threw open the nursery door. It was too sudden, no doubt. At the sight of the kettle, the rocking-horse, the tea-set, she burst into tears.

"Dear, dear Nannie," I said. "it is your own nursery; it's all from Hames."

She paused in her sobs. "The robin mug's wrong," she said, and she moved it to the opposite side of the table; "he always sat there." "He" applied to a little brother who had died, not to the mug.

"It's a very small nursery, Nannie," I said apologetically.

"Well, there are no children to make it untidy," she answered.

So Nannie and I settled down in our nursery, and through the darkening of that first evening she talked to me of my mother. It seems to me very wonderful how one woman can so devotedly love the children of another, but was it not greatly for the love of that other woman that Nannie loved us so much? It is her figure, I know, that Nannie sees when she shuts her eyes and re-peoples the nursery in her dreams,—that lovely mother, the center of that nursery and home; that mother so quick to praise, so loath to blame, so ready to find good in everything, so tender to suffering, so pitiful to sin!

"Tell me about her when she was quite young, Nannie," I said.

And Nannie talked on, telling me the stories I knew by heart and loved so dearly; and then, I remember, she started up.

"What is it, Nannie? " I asked.

"I thought she was calling," she replied; "I often seem to hear her voice."

Dear Nannie! I believe she is ready to answer that call at any moment, for all the love of her new nursery.

That is how I came to live in London.

CHAPTER VIII

Most people, I imagine, who live in London are asked by their relatives and friends who live in the country to shop for them. My post is often a matter of great anxiety to me, and I know nothing more upsetting than on a very hot summer's morning, or a wet winter's one, to find an envelope on my plate, or beside it, addressed in Cousin Anastasia's large handwriting. "Dearest," the letter inside it begins, "if" (heavily underlined) "you should be passing Paternoster Row, will you choose me a nice little prayer-book, without a cross on it, please; people tell me they are cheaper there than elsewhere, prayer-books, I mean, for Jane, who is going to be confirmed. She is such a nice clean girl. I do hope she will be as clean after her confirmation, but one never can tell. In any case I feel I ought to give her something, and a prayer-book, under the circumstances, seems the most suitable thing."

Jane, I remember, is a kitchen-maid. Of course I never pass Paternoster Row, but that to a country cousin of Anastasia's mental caliber is not worth consideration. She has no knowledge of geography, London's or otherwise, and is doubtless one of those people who think New Zealand is another name for Australia.

On another occasion she writes to say that Martha, the head housemaid, "such an excellent servant," (all heavily under lined), who has been with them seventeen years, is going to marry a nice, clean widower with six children. She must give her a nice present; "nice" is underlined several times. She has heard that in the Edgeware Road there are to be had, complete in case, for three-and-sixpence, excellent clocks. She doesn't know the name of the shop, but she believes it begins with "P," and if I could look in as I pass, she would be most grateful. As will be guessed, Anastasia is a wealthy woman with no sense of humor. She knows she has none, and she says she doesn't know what rich people want it for. Of course for poor people it is an excellent thing, because it enables them to look at the bright side of things; but as Anastasia's things, life in particular, are bright on all sides, she doesn't need that particular sense.

Then there is another country cousin she is so sweet and diffident about asking me to do anything, that I feel I ought willingly to look into every shop window in the Edgeware Road beginning with "P" or any other letter, however wet or hot the day! And I am not sure that I wouldn't! Her writing is as meek as Anastasia's is aggressive, and she never descends to the transparency of an underlined "if." She says, would I mind sending her a book, called so-and-so, by such and such an author, price so much? It is all plain sailing with Cousin Penelope. She knows just what she wants and where to get it; so much so that I sometimes wonder why she doesn't send straight to the shop. But country cousins never do that; for wherein would lie the use of London cousins, if they didn't shop for their country cousins? How would they occupy their time? She would like me please to get it at Bumpus's, because they are so very civil and they knew her dear father. I might mention his name if I thought fit! Now, I know quite well that it is impossible that any one at Bumpus's, be he ever so venerable, can ever have known Cousin Penelope's father. The name, being Smith, may no doubt be familiar. Of course Cousin Penelope would repay any expense I incurred. In fact she must insist on so doing.

"Insist" seems too strong a word to apply to any power that Cousin Penelope could enforce. It would be something so gentle; persistent, perhaps, but insistent? Never! "I beg, I implore, I entreat," would all be suitable, but "I insist " does not suggest Cousin Penelope.

Dear Cousin Penelope, we are told, had a love-story in her youth, the sadness of which ruined her life. It must have been a very beautiful thing, that sorrow., to have made her what she is. One feels that it must be a very wonderful love that is laid away in the wrappings of submission and tied with the ribbons of resignation. There is assuredly no bitterness about it, and I sometimes wonder if one's own sorrow which tears and tugs at one's heart will some day leave such a record of holiness and patience on one's face! I am afraid not. I look in the glass, but I see nothing in the reflection which in the least resembles Cousin Penelope, nor can I believe that time will do it, nor am I brave enough to wish it. I cannot yet pray for a peace like hers. People say time can do everything, but

"Time is
Too slow for those who wait,
Too swift for those who fear,
Too long for those who grieve,
Too short for those who rejoice,
But for those who love Time is
Eternity."

So it is written on a sun-dial I know, and when I have a sun-dial of my own, those words shall be written thereon.

"I think time lies heavily sometimes on Hugh's hands. He said one day, "The days pass by, Betty, and we don't grow up!"

To return to booksellers. There is "Truslove and Hanson" in my more or less immediate neighborhood, who are civil to a degree, but they did not know Cousin Penelope's father, therefore they are not specially qualified to sell a book to his daughter! So to Bumpus I must go, and I love it. A bookshop is a joy to me; the feel of books, the smell of books, the look of books, I love! I even enjoy cutting the pages of a book, which I believe every one does not enjoy.

Then there is another country cousin, Pauline. When her letter comes, I open it with mixed feelings, in which the feeling of fondness predominates. One can't help loving her. She never asks one to shop for her, but with her, which is perhaps an even greater test of friendship. On a particularly hot day, I remember, a letter came from Pauline which announced her immediate arrival. I was, waiting in the hall for her, ready to start, which is a stipulation she always makes, as she says it is such a pity to waste time. She greeted me in the same rather tempestuous manner that I am accustomed to at the hands of Betty and Hugh, and then she ran down the steps again to tell the cabman that he had a very nice horse, which she patted, and said, "Whoa, mare!" She always does that. She then asked the cabman how long he had been driving, whether it was difficult to drive at night, and whether it was true he could only see his horse's ears; and I think she asked if he had any children, but of that I am not quite sure. If she didn't, it was a lapse of memory on her part. Even the cab-runner interested her. Hadn't I noticed what a sad face he had?

I said I hadn't noticed anything except that he was rather dirty. Pauline said, "Of course he is dirty; what would you be, if you ran after cabs all day?" I wondered.

Talking of cab-runners, I told her of the children's party I went to with Cousin Penelope, who, very much afraid that she was late, said in her sweetest manner to a man who opened the cab-door for us, "Are we late?" And the man answered, "I really cannot say, madam; I have only just this moment arrived myself."

He was in rags, which I did not tell her; the sponge cake would have stuck in her throat at tea if I had. But I gave him something for his ready wit, and wished for weeks afterwards that I had plunged into the darkness after him. "What a charming man!" said Cousin Penelope. But to return to Pauline.

"What a glorious day we are going to have!" she said. "It is good of you to say I may stay the night, and if I go to a ball, you won't mind? I have brought a small box,—as you see."

I did see, and to my mind its size bordered on indecency. I like a box to look sufficiently large to take all I think a woman ought to need for a night's stay. Pauline often assures me it does hold everything, squashed tight, of course. I say it must be squashed very tight, and she says it is. "That's the beauty of the present-day fashion of fluffy things: everything is so easily squashed, and yet you can't squash them; an accordion-pleated thing, for instance."

To a man whose admiration for a woman is gauged by the amount of luggage she can travel without, Pauline would prove irresistible. I know one who prides himself on his packing, and who has a horror of much luggage. He was all packed ready to go to Scotland, when his wife asked him if he could lend her a collar-stud for her flannel shirts, and he said, "Yes, but you must carry it yourself, I'm full up!"

To that man Pauline, I am sure, would be very attractive.

When Pauline and I started off on our shopping expedition, she demurred at taking a hansom, although she loves driving in them; but she said 'buses were so much more amusing. People in 'buses say such funny things," she said, and so they do. The old lady in particular who, when the horse got his leg over the trace without hurting himself or any one else, got up and announced to the 'bus in general: "There, I always did say I hated horses and dogs," and sat down again. I loved her for that and for other things too, among them her apple-cheeks and poke bonnet.

Another reason why I insisted upon a hansom is that Pauline is not to be trusted in a 'bus; her interest in her fellow-creatures is embarrassing. I have, moreover, sat opposite babies in 'buses with Pauline, and where a baby is concerned, she has no self-control. So I was firm, and we started off in a hansom. I was continually besought to look at some delicious baby, first this side, then that.

Pauline calmly avers that she would go mad if she lived in London. She couldn't stand seeing so many beautiful children, or babies, beautiful or otherwise. It is curious how babies in perambulators hold out their hands to Pauline as she passes, and laugh andgurgle at her.

Once in Piccadilly, beautiful babies became less plentiful, and Pauline turned her thoughts and sympathies to horses and bearing-reins. She was instantly plunged into the depths of despair. Couldn't I do something, she asked, to remedy such a crying evil? She said it was the duty of every woman in London—Something in the catalogue she was carrying arrested her attention, and what it was the duty of every woman to do I am not sure. I did not ask, but was grateful for the peace which ensued.

Pauline was glad the sales were on. She loved them, and yet she didn't like them, because she didn't think they brought out the best side of a woman's character. "I think," she said, "a woman's behavior at sales is a test, don't you?"

I said I thought her behavior as regarded swing-doors was a surer one. She said she hadn't thought of that.

"But I know what you mean; I do dislike the flouncing, push-ing woman. I think every one should be taught to be courteous and gentle, don't you?" She added, "I hate being pushed."

I told her of a woman next me in a 'bus one day, who said, "You're a-sittin' on me!" How I rose and politely begged her pardon, whereupon she said, "Now you're a-standin' on me!" And we agreed that there is no pleasing some people.

Pauline returned to the perusal of the catalogue, in which she had put a large cross against the picture of a coat and skirt. She said she was stock-size. She didn't suppose any really smart women were. "Or would own to it," I suggested, but she didn't answer; she never does if she detects any savor of malice in a remark. She was very anxious I should admire the illustration.

I did, but I felt it my duty as a London cousin to a country cousin to tell her that the illustration might lead her to expect too much. She warmly agreed that of course as regarded the figure, etc., the illustration was misleading, because she, of course, could never look so beautifully willowy as that. She was inclined to come out where the illustration went in, and she could never be so slanty, never; but apart from that, of course the coat and skirt would be exactly as it was pictured. Her figure would be to blame, of course. Her figure happens to be a very pretty one, but she didn't give me time to say so. I repeated that I should not put implicit faith in the illustration. She was a little hurt. She did not think it right to cast aspersions on the character of so respectable a firm as that whose name headed the catalogue. I said I didn't see it quite in the same light. Pauline looked at me reproachfully, and said drawing a lie was as bad as telling one.

The argument was beyond me; besides, I like Pauline to look reproachfully at me, she is so pretty. Being as pretty as she undoubtedly is, I often wonder why she is not more effective.

The right kind of country beauty is very convincing to the jaded Londoner; but to convince, one must be convinced, and that is exactly what Pauline is not. She never thinks whether she is beautiful or not, and I am sure it often lies with the woman herself, how beautiful people think her, except in the rare cases of real beauty, when there can be but one opinion. But in the case of ordinary beauty, the woman is appraised at her own value. Then there is the art of putting on clothes, of which Pauline is absolutely ignorant. There is even a studied untidiness which passes under the name of picturesque. All of this is a closed book to Pauline, and, after all, she is a delightful creature; but the trouble to me was that, at the time she came up to shop with me, she didn't wear good boots, and to do that I hold is part, or should be part, of a woman's creed. She gets her. boots from the village shoemaker because his wife died. Her eyes filled with tears at the mere thought of the man, and she told me she thought it right to encourage local talent. In the boots I saw evidences of locality,—bumps, for instance,—but not of talent. Pauline was very indignant and said she had no bumps on her feet. "But you see my position?" I did, but I persuaded her to have some good boots made in London. This she consented to do, rather unwillingly and on the distinct understanding that in the country she should continue to encourage local talent. On wet days," I ventured.

And at flower-shows, she added.

I have seen Pauline in the country, against a background of golden beech trees and brown bracken, look even beautiful; but in London she lacks something, possibly the right background. She has glorious hair, but her maid can't do it. Pauline admits it, but she says she can't send a nice woman away on that account; besides, she suffers from rheumatism, and Pauline's particular part of the country suits her better than any other.

"Couldn't she learn?" I suggested.

"No, she can't," said Pauline. "She had lessons once, and she came back and did my hair like treacle, all over my head,—no idea, absolutely. I should never look like you, whatever I did."

"My dear Pauline," I said, "what nonsense!"

"It's not nonsense. Father was saying only the other day that you are a beautiful creature, only no one seems to see it."

"Dear Uncle Jim," I said; "how delightful, and how like him!"

"But it's true you are beautiful; only the part about the people not seeing it isn't true: that's father's way of putting it. You are beautiful!"

"My dear child!"

"Why do you say 'dear child' to me? People would think you were years and years older than I am. Why do you always talk as if life were over? Have you a secret sorrow?"

If Pauline, warm-hearted, loving Pauline had really thought I had, she would have been the last person to ask such a question.

"Do I look it?" I asked.

"No-o. Only when people seem to spend the whole of their life in doing things for other people, it makes one suspect that they are saying to themselves, 'As we can't be happy ourselves, we can see that other people are.'"

"What a philosopher you are, Pauline! If you go on that supposition, you must have a terrible sorrow somewhere hidden behind that happy face of yours."

Pauline is not meant to live in London. She thanks people in a crowd for letting her pass. If she is pushed off the pavement, she is only sorry that the person can be so rude as to do it . She never gets into a 'bus or takes any vehicular advantage over a widow, and she feels choky if she sees any one very old. "Do you know why?" she asked. "Because they are, so near Heaven, and sometimes I think you see the reflection of it in their faces."

"Like Cousin Penelope," I said.

We arrived at the shop where the coat and skirt were to be had, and Pauline, having admired the horse and thanked the cabman, and the commissionaire, who held his arm over a perfectly dry wheel, followed me into the shop. She admired everything as she went through the different departments, and apologized to the shop walkers for not being able to buy everything; but she lived in the country, and although the things were lovely, they would be no use to her—dogs on her lap most of the day, and so on.

Everyone looked at Pauline; and old ladies, to whom she

Mary C.E. Wemyss

always appeals very much, put their heads on one side, as old ladies do when they admire anything very much, anything which reminds them of their own youth, and smiled. Old ladies have this privilege, that when they arrive at a certain age, they are allowed to think they were beautiful in their youth, and to tell you so. It is a recognized thing, and one of the recompenses of old age. We all know that every one had a beautiful grandmother—one at least; and if a portrait of one grandmother belies the fact, then there is the other one to fall back upon, of whom, unfortunately, no portrait exists, and she was abs—so—lute—lee lovely!

The coat and skirt were found and eagerly compared with the illustration, and Pauline turned to me and said with a triumphant ringing her voice: "It wasn't an exaggeration. I knew it wouldn't be. Mother has dealt here for years."

Then we went upstairs to try it on. In a few minutes Pauline had discovered that the fitter was supporting her deceased sister's husband and six children, the eldest of whom wasn't quite right and the youngest had rickets. She was so distressed that she didn't want the back of her coat altered, the woman already had so much to bear. But I prevailed upon her to have the alteration made regardless of the woman's domestic anxieties. I felt sure it would make no difference. But I cannot help feeling that Pauline's visit to that shop did make a difference to that poor woman, if only for a few moments in her life. And I think those children's lives were made happier too; but it is difficult to get Pauline to talk of these things.

Then we went to the shoemaker, and Pauline told him all about the widower bootmaker, and of her scruples about having boots made by any one else. The bootmaker evidently thought that a foot like Pauline's was worthy of a good boot and Pauline said there were occasions on which one had to sink one's own feelings. She was scandalized at London prices, and told the man so. "But of course it means higher pay for the men, so it's all right."

On our way home I said to Pauline that I couldn't understand why she was so economical—ready-made coats and skirts, and afraid of paying a fair price for good boots! Was her allowance smaller than it used to be? She got pink and didn't answer. I determined she should, and at last she did.

"Well, you see, I pay a woman to come and wash the shoemaker's children on Saturday evenings."

I smiled. "That can't cost much, unless she provides the soap."

Pauline got pinker still. "Well, I pay for the village nurse, and a few other little things. Then there's a little baby," she dropped her voice, "who has no mother—she died—and who never had a father, and every one doesn't care for those sort of babies. —You do like my coat and skirt, don't you?"

CHAPTER IX

I think, by the way, that it was on that very day that Mr. Dudley met Pauline. She, of course, would know the exact date and hour, but I am almost sure of it, for although it may mean a day of less ecstatic joy to me than it does to her, it brought much peace and subsequent happiness into my life, and therefore is writ in red letters in my book of days. For the visits of Dick Dudley had latterly become more frequent than I cared for, and much as I liked him, I began to wish that I had remained in his estimation under the shadow of Diana's charming personality, for so he had tolerated me until the fateful day on which I had partaken of Betty's gray wad. That act of professional valor ignited a spark of feeling for me in his breast, which, fostered by Hugh's constant suggestion, sprang into something warmer than I could have wished, and was fanned into flame on the day on which he found me paying a visit of consolation to the small fat Thomas. Now, strangely enough, that small fat person was nephew to Dick Dudley. How small the world is! And the mother turned out to have been exactly the sort of mother I had thought she must be. One of the nicest things about Dick Dudley was the way he spoke of that sister) and we had long talks about her, until I awoke to the fact that that sister and I must have been twins, so alike were we; then I began to be afraid. For I couldn't tell him that there was some one far away, for whom I was waiting from day to day. One can hardly barricade one's self behind such an announcement. The classification of women is incomplete. There are those who are engaged and who care; there are those who are engaged and who don't care; there are those who don't care and, who are not engaged; then there are those who care and who are not engaged, so cannot say. It is not their fault if, sometimes, they wound a passing lover. Mercifully there are Pauline's in this world to relieve one of unsought affections, and I liked Dick Dudley well enough, and not too much to be glad when I saw him give ever such a small start when he walked into my drawing-room and saw Pauline sitting there, clothed in cool green linen and looking her very best. I had done her glorious hair on the top—that, I think is the expression—and she sat in the window so that her hair shone like burnished gold, and she was saying in a voice fraught with emotion, "If I had my way, there should be no sorrow or suffering," which of all sentiments was the most likely to appeal to Dick Dudley, for he is one of those who look upon sorrow and suffering as bad management on the part of some one, since the world is really such an awfully jolly place, if only people didn't make a muddle of their lives. He says it is all very well to talk of high ideals, you can't live up to them, the best you can do is to live up to the highest practical ideal. But then his standard of ideal is very much higher since he saw Pauline for the first time. Pauline blushed when a strange man walked into the room, which was all for the best, and made the day a happier one for me. Not that Dick Dudley was not very loyal to me. He tried, I could see it was an effort) not to talk too much to Pauline, although the topic of bearing-reins, under certain circumstances, was a very engrossing one, and spaniels a never-ending one. Pauline expressed her surprise that Mr. Dudley should ask her if she lived in London.

"I thought every one could see I lived in the country," she said. "Did you mean it for a compliment?" she asked kindly.

Dick Dudley was a little overcome by this, and he said he would hardly have dared to pay her a compliment, since every one knew that girls who lived in the country away from bearing-reins and other hardening and worldly influences, and in close proximity to spaniels, black, liver and white, cocker, clumber, and otherwise, were so vastly superior to their London sisters. Here Dick got a little deep and Pauline kindly

Mary C.E. Wemyss

rescued him.

"A compliment to my clothes, I meant," she said; "because all my friends in London tell me my clothes are so countrified."

Dick listened very, very seriously to the reasons why Pauline was obliged to have most of her clothes made in the country, and I could see that every moment he thought less of the importance of clothes and their makers, and more and more of the qualities essential in woman, simplicity, goodness, frankness, and an absence of artificiality. I saw it all on his face, dawning slowly and surely. By the time we had had tea, I could see it was a matter of mutual satisfaction to both Dick and Pauline to find that they were going to the same dance that night. The responsibility of chaperoning Pauline was not mine.

My anxiety as to the ball dress emerging from the small box was relieved by Pauline telling me that it was to come from the dressmaker just in time for her to dress for the ball; which it did. She came to be inspected by Nannie and me before she started, and she really looked delicious. Her assets as a country girl counted heavily that night, she looked so fresh, so natural, and so full of the joy of living. Her hair counted, every hair of it. Nannie was so touched that she wept aloud and said it was what I ought to be doing. But I told her professional aunts went only to children's parties, where they could be of some use. Pauline wished I was going. "Betty," she said and paused, I am sure Mr.—is his name Dudley? feels very much your not going." I laughed, and marked it down against her that she should have said, "Is his name Dudley?" It was the first evidence of feminine guile I had detected in her. Men are answerable for a very great deal.

I woke to greet Pauline when she came into my sunlit room at five o'clock in the morning, looking still fresh, untired, and more than ever full of the joy of living. "Oh, it was lovely," she said, sitting down on my bed.

"Who saw you home?" I asked professionally.

"Oh, Aunt Adela to the very door; she even waited till I shut it."

"Who did you dance with? " I asked.

"Heaps and heaps of people. I was lucky; all Thorpshire seemed to be there; and then Mr. Dudley. Betty, I understand now."

"What?" I said, alarmed by the note of tragic kindness in her voice.

"About Mr. Dudley, he talked about you so beautifully. He agrees with me absolutely about your character, and he told me about his sister." Pauline's voice became hushed.

"Did he say she was just a little like you, Pauline?"

"Yes, he did. You knew her, then? He said I reminded him of her so strangely. I think he would make a woman very happy. I do really."

"So do I, dear Pauline, really."

"Then won't you?"

"No, darling goose."

"Why?"

"Because I am not the woman. Go to bed, Pauline."

She went—to sleep? I cannot say. I forget whether a girl goes to sleep the first night after she has fallen in love. Night? I suppose I should say morning. But it depends on the hour when she takes the first step into that bewildering fairyland of first love. For a fairyland it assuredly is, if she is lucky enough to find the right guide. He must, to begin with, believe in the fairyland. He must know that the path may be rough at times, stony and overgrown with weeds, but he will know that all the difficulties will be worth while when he brings her out into the open, and they look away to the limitless horizon of happiness.

A few hours later, Pauline said to me at breakfast, "Betty, I think I shall tell that bootmaker to make me two pairs of boots and two pairs of shoes. It is better to have enough while one is about it, don't you think so?"

So began the regeneration of Pauline, regeneration in the matter of footgear, I mean, and to wear good boots did her character no harm, nor the pocket of the country shoemaker either, I am sure. Good boots could not turn her feet from the pathway of truth and goodness which from her earliest childhood she had set out to tread, never pausing except to pick up some one who lagged behind, or to help some one who had strayed from the path.

Dick Dudley, whose pathway through life had zigzagged considerably, was astonished to find how easy the pathway was to keep, guided by Pauline, and how alluring the goal of goodness. He gave himself up gladly to her guidance, and was touched to find how much there was of latent goodness in him. He had never before realized, that was all, how much he loved his fellow-creatures, how he longed to help them all, how the conditions of the laboring-classes made his blood boil with indignation, how he idolized babies, loved old women, reverenced old men.

It was all a revelation to him. It was, moreover, delightful to be told by Pauline how wonderful she found all these things in him, and how unexpected. This, she explained, was nothing personal. "But I often wondered if I should ever meet a man like you."

"Darling," he answered humbly, "I don't think I am that sort of man; really, I'm awfully and frightfully ordinary."

Then Pauline, to prove the contrary, would ask him if he

didn't feel this or that or the other? And of course he could truthfully say he did, because he felt all and everything Pauline wished him to feel, with her beautiful eyes fixed upon him and the flush of enthusiasm on her cheeks. Here was something to inspire a man, this splendidly generous, magnanimous creature. Of course he had always felt all these things; he had been groping after goodness. It was the goodness in Diana, and he was kind enough to say in the professional aunt, which had appealed to him. He had been feeling after, it for years, but it was only Pauline who had revealed it to him, in himself. Well, he was very much in love. Most men engaged to charming girls feel their own unworthiness, and the girl is sweetly content that they should do so. Not so Pauline. She revealed to her astonished lover a depth of goodness in his character that he had least suspected, and he gradually began to feel how little he had been understood.

Now this is an excellent basis on which to start an engagement. I forget exactly how and when they became engaged, but it was certainly before Dick said humbly, "Darling, I don't think I am that sort of man; really, I'm awfully and frightfully ordinary," because, with all Pauline's kindness to sinners, there was none hardened enough to address her as "darling" without being first engaged to her; so by that I know they were engaged that evening at the opera, because it was in a Wagnerian pause that Dick said those words, in a loud voice from the back of the box. How else should a professional aunt know these things?

Between meeting Dick and becoming engaged to him, Pauline went home and came back with a larger box and stayed quite a long time, as time goes, although, as a time in which to become engaged, it was very short, and Nannie, feeling this, asked Pauline if she knew much about Mr. Dudley, and was she wise? In spite of this anxiety on Nannie's part, she enjoyed it all immensely, and wept to her heart's content when the engagement was announced. Now Dick Dudley was a rich young man, and I wondered whether other people wept too from motives less pure and simple than Nannie's.

Pauline wanted me to join a society called "The Deaf Dog Society." The obligation enforced on members was that they should kneel down, put their arms round the neck of any deaf dog they should chance to meet, and say, "Darling, I love you."

"You see," she said, "a deaf dog doesn't know he is deaf, he only wonders why no one ever speaks to him, why no one ever calls him. So you see what a splendid society it is, and there is no subscription."

Dick made a stipulation that the benefits of the society should be conferred on dogs only. He made a point of that.

CHAPTER X

As there was nothing to wait for, happy people, it was agreed by all parties that the wedding should take place in August, which kept me rather late in town; it was hardly worth going away, to come back again, as back again I had to come, as Betty and Hugh were coming to stay with me for a night on their way to Thorpshire. It is not astonishing, perhaps, that two children, modern children in particular, and a nursery-maid can fill to overflowing a small London house, but it is astonishing how demoralizing a thing it is. A visiting child to people who have children of their own means nothing, beyond the changing from one room to another of some particular child, or the putting up of an extra bed, or perhaps the joy supreme to some child of sleeping in something that is not a real bed. We all remember that joy. Except for that one child, it is an every-day thing and fraught with no particular excitement. The servants, for instance, in a house where children are an every-day thing, remain quite calm, if good tempered, when a visiting child is expected, and the kitchen-maid, no doubt, cleans the doorstep as usual, and, no doubt, takes in the milk. But this I know, that if I had happened to possess such a thing when Betty and Hugh were coming to stay, my doorstep would never have been cleaned. For once I was glad that I depended on the services of a very small boy, who thinks he cleans it. Staid and level-headed as were my maids, they answered no bells that morning, which was perhaps natural, as I believe none ring up to the nursery. Of course they had to be interested in Nannie's arrangements.

Mary C.E. Wemyss

It was a hot August day, I remember, and I sat at the window writing, or pretending to write. As a matter of fact, I was listening. Among other things to the "Austrian Anthem," played over and over again, first right hand, then left, then both, but not together, by, I guessed, a child about ten years old, next door.

Poor, hot child, how I pitied her.

"Never mind," I thought, "take courage, seaside time is coming. Within a few days, no doubt, an omnibus will come to the door empty, to go away full, filled with luggage, crowned by a perambulator and a baby's bath!" It is only a woman who can travel with a perambulator and a bath; they are the epitome of motherhood. A father is always too busy to go by that particular train.

I heard the twitter of sparrows, the jingle of bells, the hooting of a siren, or was it my neighbor singing "A rose I gave to you"? of course it was,—the rumble of a post-office van, and the cry of children's voices, rather peevish voices, poor mites! Never mind, seaside time is coming.

Listening more intently, I beard in the far distance, yet distinct, the cries of the children who ought to go to the seaside, children who have never been to the seaside, never paddled, never built castles, never caught crabs, never seen sea-anemones or starfish, children whose faces are wan and whose mothers are too tired to be kind to them. It is often that, I am sure, too tired to be kind!

Listening again, I heard faintly—it is not with the ears that one hears these things—the unuttered complaints of those tired mothers, worn-out women, despairing men, and the singing, in dark alleys and in hot areas, of caged birds. There are thousands of caged creatures, other than birds, in London in August, men, women, and children. Hats off, then, to the little feathered Christians who sing for their fellow-prisoners a paean of praise. It is perhaps easier to sing to the patch of blue sky when you do not know that it will be hidden behind clouds tomorrow.

"They've come," cried Nannie.

"O Aunt Woggles!" said Hugh, "I've brought you a lovely caterpillar wrapped up in grass."

"And I've brought you one of my very own bantam eggs," said Betty. "I've kept it ever so long for you."

Then it will be bad, said Hugh.

"Oh, not so long as to be bad," said Betty. "You will eat it, won't you, Aunt Woggles?"

Nannie was radiantly happy at tea that day, but I think her happiness was supreme when she fetched me later to look at the children asleep. We stole into Betty's room together, and Nannie shaded the candle as she held it, for me to look at what is assuredly the loveliest thing on God's earth—a sleeping child.

Nannie, in an eloquent silence, pointed to the chair on which lay Betty's clean clothes, folded ready for the morning, and to her hairy horse which she had brought for company. Her blue slippers were beside the bed. Then we went into Hugh's room. He, too, lay peaceful and beautiful, his clothes folded ready for the morning, and his pistol beside him in case he was "attacked." His slippers were red, and Nannie, at the sight of them, cried quietly. To some happy mothers a child's slippers mean nothing more than size two or three, and serve only to remind her how quickly children grow out of things!

But to Nannie they brought back memories of years of happiness, through which little feet, in just the same sort of slippers, had pattered, stumbling here, falling there, picked up, and guided by her. But she thought most of the little feet in just that sort of slippers, that had stopped still forever early on their life's journey. It is the voices that are hushed that call most distinctly, the footsteps that stop that are most carefully traced. It is the children who have gone that stand and beckon!

CHAPTER XI

Pauline's wedding-day dawned gloriously bright and beautiful. The whole village was up and doing, very early, putting the finishing touches to the decorations.

The widower shoemaker and his children, and the woman who washed them—the children, I mean—on Saturdays, had all combined to erect a triumphal arch of, great splendor, and the woman showed such sensibility in the choice of mottoes, and such a nice appreciation of the joys of matrimony, together with a decided leaning towards the bridegroom's side of the arch, that the shoemaker suggested that she should suit her actions to her words—that was how he expressed it—and marry him, which she agreed to do. But she afterwards explained, in breaking the news to her friends, that they could have knocked her down with a leaf! Whether this was due to the weakened state of her heart, or to her precarious position on the ladder, I do not know.

Everybody and everything was in a bustle, with the exception of Aunt Cecilia, who sat through it all as calm and as beautiful as ever. Not that she did not feel parting with Pauline, but her love for everybody and everything was of a nature so purely unselfish that it never occurred to her to count the cost to herself.

I have never met any one who so completely combines in her character gentleness and strength as does Aunt Cecilia: so gentle in spirit and judgment, and so strong in her fight for

Mary C.E. Wemyss

principles and beliefs. If she has a weakness, and I could never wish any one I love to be without one, it lies in her love for Patience. She does not think it right to play in the morning, but sometimes, being unable to withstand the temptation of so doing, she plays it in an empty drawer of her writing-table, and if she hears any one coming, she can close the drawer!

Her greatest interest in life, next to her husband and children, is her garden and other people's gardens. In fact, she looks at life generally from a gardening point of view, and is apt to regard men as gardeners, possible gardeners, or gardeners wasted. As gardeners they have their very distinct use, and as such deserve every consideration, but if a man will not till the soil, he is a cumberer thereof. She, at least, inclines that way in thought. Life, she says, is a garden, children the flowers, parents the gardeners. "If we treated children as we do roses, they would be far happier. We don't call roses naughty when they grow badly and refuse to flower as they ought to; we blame the gardeners or the soil."

"But, Aunt Cecilia," I say, "one can recommend an unsatisfactory gardener to a friend, but one can't so dispose of unsatisfactory parents."

"You must educate them, dear."

Now all this sounds very convincing when said by Aunt Cecilia, because, for one thing, she says it very charmingly, and for another, she is still a very beautiful woman. She is too fond, perhaps, of extinguishing her beauty under a large mushroom hat, and is given to bending too much over herbaceous borders, and so hiding her beautiful face. But I dare say the flowers love to look at it, and to see mirrored in it their own loveliness.

Aunt Cecilia wears a bonnet sometimes, and thereby hangs a tale. So few aunts wear a bonnet nowadays that the fact of one doing so is almost worth chronicling. She doesn't wear it very often, only at the christenings of the head gardener's babies.

From a christening point of view that is very often, but from a bonnet point of view I suppose it might be called seldom— once a year? I know that bonnet well, because it has been sent to me often for renovation. On one particular occasion it arrived in a cardboard box. On the top of the bonnet was a bunch of flowers, beautiful enough to make any bonnet accompanying it welcome, in whatever state of dilapidation. Aunt Cecilia has a knack of sending just the right sort of flowers, and they always bring a message, which everybody's flowers don't do.

The bonnet I renovated to the best of my ability and sent it back. In the course of a few days I received a slightly agitated note from Aunt Cecilia. "It doesn't suit me, dearest, and after all the trouble you have taken!"

Knowing Aunt Cecilia, I wrote back, "Did you try it on in bed with your hair down?"

She answered by return, "Dearest, I did! It really suits me very well now that I have tried it on in my right mind. I am going to wear it at the last little Shrub's christening, this afternoon. It is just in time."

When David and Diana were singled out by night for the particular attention of a burglar, Aunt Cecilia wrote to sympathize and said, "I am so thankful, dearest, David did not meet the poor, misguided man!"

May we all be judged as tenderly!

This is a digression, but it perhaps explains Pauline and Pauline's wedding, and the joy with which all the people in the village entered into it.

The strangest people kept on arriving the morning of the wedding. It was verily a gathering of the halt, the lame, and the blind—all friends of Pauline's. Whenever Uncle Jim was particularly overcome, it was sure to mean that some old

Mary C.E. Wemyss

soldier, officer or otherwise, had turned up, who had served with him in some part of the world, long before Pauline was born. Aunt Cecilia welcomed them all in her inimitable manner, which made each one feel that he was the one and most particularly honored guest. For all her apparent absent-mindedness, she knew exactly who belonged to Mrs. Bunce's department and who not.

Mrs. Bunce, the old housekeeper, was very busy, every button doing its duty! A wedding didn't come her way every day. The sisters-in-law, of course, came with their belongings.

Zerlina was distressed at the nature of many of the presents; and wondered if Pauline would have enough spare rooms to put them in; which showed how little she knew her. If Pauline had told her that she valued the alabaster greyhound under a glass case, subscribed for by the old men and women in the village, over seventy, Zerlina wouldn't have believed her any more than did old Mrs. Barker when Diana told her Sara was named after a dear old housemaid and not after the Duchess.

Betty and Hugh were among the bridesmaids and pages, and Hugh shocked Betty very much by saying, in the middle of the service "When may I play with my girl?"

Some one described Uncle Jim as looking like one of the Apostles, and Aunt Cecilia certainly looked like a saint. Ought I, by the way, to bracket an apostle and a saint? But nothing was so wonderful or so beautiful as the expression on Pauline's face. I am sure that, as she walked up the aisle, she was oblivious to everything and every one except God and Dick.

It is assuredly a great responsibility for a man to accept such a love as hers.

A wedding is nearly always a choky thing, and Pauline's was particularly so. As she left the church, she stopped in the churchyard to speak to her friends, and for one old woman she waited to let her feel her dress.

"Is it my jewels you want to feel, Anne?" she said, as the old hands tremblingly passed over her bodice. "I have on no jewels."

The old hands went up to Pauline's face and gently and reverently touched it. "God bless her happy face," said the old woman. "I had to know for sure." Pauline kissed the old fingers gently. We all knew for sure, but then we had eyes to see.

Pauline went away in the afternoon, and the villagers danced far into the evening, and there was revelry in the park by night.

After Pauline and Dick had gone away, I walked across the park to the post office to send a telegram to Julia, who was kept at home by illness, to her very great disappointment. There is nothing she adores like a wedding. I was glad to escape for a few minutes. I wrote out the telegram and handed it to the postmaster, who, reading it, said, I'm glad it went off so well. "There's nobody what wouldn't wish her well." Then he counted the words. "Julia Westby?" he said. "Um-um-um-um. Eleven, miss. You might as well give her the title." I laughed and added, or rather he added, the "Lady."

Julia is not a sister-in-law really, but she likes to call herself so, since she might have been one, having been for one ecstatic week in Archie's life engaged to him. She is wont now to lay her hand on his head, in public, for choice, and say, "He was almost mine." She says she still loves him as a friend. "But, you see, dearest Betty, there is everything that is delightful in the relationship of a poor friend, but a poor husband! That is another thing. To begin with, it is not fair to a man that he should have to deny his wife things. It is bad for his character and, of course, for hers. He becomes a saint at her expense, whereas the expense should always be borne by the husband. William is so delightfully rich, but he is not an Archie, of course! But then husbands are not supposed to be."

Hugh, going to bed, wondered if the angels would bring

Pauline a baby that night, a darling little baby!

And Betty said, in her great wisdom, "Oh, darling, I think it would be too exciting for Pauline to be married and have a baby all on one day."

Then Hugh suggested the glorious possibility of the angels bringing it to Fullfield, whereupon Hyacinth said that was not at all likely, because she knew that when a baby was born, it was usual for one or other parent to be present!

We stayed for a few days at Fullfield, and Hugh and Betty enjoyed themselves immensely. Hyacinth said it was just like staying for a week at the pantomime, and Betty said, with a deep sigh, that it was much nicer, a billion times nicer.

Pauline's brother Jack most nearly resembled any one in a pantomime, and the children loved him. One day at lunch he went to the side-table to fetch a potato in its jacket, and coming back he laid it on Uncle Jim's slightly bald head and said, "Am I feverish, father?"

"It Good Heavens, my boy!" exclaimed Uncle Jim; "you must be in an awful state!"

After that, the eyes of the children never left Jack during any meal at which they happened to be present, and whenever he got up to fetch anything, Hugh began dancing with joy and saying in a loud whisper, "He's going to do something funny"; and if Jack remained silent, Hugh was sure he was thinking of something to do. It is difficult to live up to those expectations.

One morning at breakfast Hugh said suddenly, "Aunt Woggles, have you got a mole?"

I said I believed I had.

"It's frightfully lucky. I have," he said, pulling up his sleeve and disclosing a mole on his very white little arm. "It is lucky."

"I've got one too," said Betty, diving under the table.

"All right, darling," I said, "you needn't show us."

"I couldn't, Aunt Woggles, at least not now. If you come to see me in my bath, you can; but it's truthfully there."

I said I was sure it was.

"I 'spect she's sitting on it," said Hugh in a loud whisper; "that's why."

"We asked Mr. Hardy once if he had a mole, and he got redder and redder;" we asked him at lunch, said Betty.

"He got redder and redder," said Hugh, by way of corroboration. "Mother said moles weren't good things to ask people about, so we asked him if he had any little children, and he hadn't; then we didn't know what to ask."

"We only asked about moles because we wanted him to be lucky," said kindhearted Betty.

"Last time I went to the Zoo," said Hugh, "I gave all my bread to one animal. He was a lucky animal, wasn't he?"

It was the hippopotamus, I think; he was lucky."

"Perhaps he has a mole, Hugh," I said.

We'll look, said Hugh. "I 'spect he has."

The proverbial difficulty of finding a needle in a haystack seemed child's play compared to that of finding a mole on a hippopotamus.

CHAPTER XII

Another aunt, Anna by name, suggested that as I was at Fullfield, I might take the opportunity of paying her a visit at Manwell, why because I was at Fullfield I don't know, as they are miles apart, counties apart I should say. However, I went because it is difficult to refuse Aunt Anna anything; she accepts no excuses. It is as well for any one who wishes to see Aunt Anna at her best to see her in her own home. She, according to Aunt Cecilia, does best in her own soil. Moreover, she is nothing without her family, it so thoroughly justifies her existence.

Aunt Anna is one of those jewels who owe a certain amount to their setting.

Her husband calls her a jewel, and as such she is known by the family in general which recalls to my mind an interesting biennial custom which was said to hold good in the Manwell family. Every time a lesser jewel made its appearance, the mother-jewel was presented with a diamond and ruby ornament of varying magnificence, with the words "The price of a good woman is far above rubies" conveniently inscribed thereon.

Aunt Anna took it all very seriously, from the tiara downward, and if diamond and ruby shoe-buckles had not involved twins, I think she would have hankered after those, but even as it was, she came in time to possess a very remarkable collection of rubies and diamonds.

Aunt Anna is very prosperous, very happy, very rich, and very contented.

She prides herself on none of these things, but only on the unprejudiced state of her maternal mind.

"Of course," she says, "I cannot help seeing that my children are more beautiful than other people's. It would be ludicrously affected and hypocritical of me if I pretended otherwise. If they were plain, I should be the first to see it, and—"

I think she was going to add "say it," but she stopped short; she invariably does at a deliberate lie, because she is a very truthful woman, and thinks a lie is a wicked thing unless socially a necessity.

I arrived at tea-time which is a thing Aunt Anna expects of her guests. I noticed that she looked a little less contented than usual, and that she even gave way to a gesture of impatience when Mrs. Blankley asked for a fifth cup of tea. Mrs. Blankley is a great advocate of temperance. In connection with which, Aunt Anna once said that she thought there should be temperance in all things beginning with "t." Which vague saying, as illustrative of her wit, was treasured up by her indulgent husband and quoted "As Anna so funnily said."

Now as Aunt Anna, we know, never says witty things unless under strong provocation, she rarely says them, for she is of an amazingly even temperament. She often says she considers cleverness a very dangerous gift. It is not one I seek for either myself or my children. It is so easy to say clever, unkind things. Every one can do it if they choose; the difficulty is not to say them.

It is evident that Aunt Anna chooses the harder part.

Mrs. Blankley, having disposed of the fifth cup of tea, expressed a desire to see the pigs. Aunt Anna never goes to see pigs, nor demands that sacrifice of Londoners, for which act of consideration I honor her; not but what I am fond of pigs, black ones and small. Aunt Anna knows that there are such things because of the continual presence of bacon in her midst. She also knows that pigs are things that get prizes. She still clings to her childish belief that streaky bacon comes from feeding the pigs one day and not the next.

Every one, like Mrs. Blankley, had a thirst to see something, and I was left alone with Aunt Anna, to discuss Pauline's wedding. As a rule, there is nothing Aunt Anna would sooner discuss, but I saw that something was worrying her, and I guessed that the unburdening of a rarely perturbed mind was imminent. It was.

"Is anything wrong?—I asked. "Any of the children worrying you? She nodded and pointed to a diamond and ruby brooch and said plaintively. "This one, Claud, just a little worrying."

I tried to hide a smile. "Oh, that's Claud, is it? I get a little mixed."

"I dare say, dear," she said; "but it's quite simple, really. Jack was the tiara, and so on."

"What has Claud been doing?" I asked. "Oh, nothing he can help, I feel sure. He has a temperament, I believe. What it is I don't quite know; people grow out of it, I am told. It's not so much doing things as saying them; and his friends are odd, decidedly odd. They wear curious ties, have disheveled hair, and are distinctly décolleté. I don't know if I should apply the word to men, but they are."

I suggested that these little indiscretions on the part of extreme youth need not worry her. But she said they did, in a way, because her other children were so very plain sailing. They never took any one by surprise. She then told me of poor Lady Adelaide, a near neighbor, at least as near as it was possible for any neighbor to be, considering the extent of the Manwell property, one of whose boys had written a book without her knowledge, and the other had married under exactly similar conditions.

I said I thought the writing of a book a minor offense compared to the matrimonial venture. She agreed, but said they were both upsetting because unexpected. As an instance, did I remember when Lady Victoria was butted by her pet lamb, when she was showing the Prince her white farm? It wasn't the upsetting she minded, so much as the unexpectedness of it, because the lamb had a blue ribbon round its neck!

"A black sheep in a white farm, Aunt Anna!" I said.

"No, dear, it was white, and it was a lamb."

But to return to Lady Adelaide. Now that Aunt Anna came to think of it, the marriage was the better of the two shocks, because financially it was a success, and the book wasn't. "Books aren't," She added.

"Is that all Claud does, or, rather, his friends do?" I asked.

"No, it's not," she said. "Ever since he went to Oxford he has changed completely. He has got into his head that we are a self-centered family, and that I am a prejudiced mother, when it is the only thing I am not. I may be everything else for all I know, I may be daily breaking all the commandments without knowing it! But a prejudiced mother I am not! Before he went to Oxford he came into my bedroom one morning, and he said that he thought Maud and Edith were quite the most beautiful girls he had ever seen, and he had sat behind some famous beauty in a theatre a few nights before. I didn't ask him! I was suffering from neuralgia at the time, I remember, and he might, under the circumstances, have agreed just to soothe me, but he said it of his own accord, and he wondered if they would go up to London and walk down Bond Street with him. I said it should be arranged. They walked with him three times up and down Bond Street; he only asked for once.

Mary C.E. Wemyss

I am only telling you this because you will then realize what this change in him means to me. He came back from Oxford after one term and he said nothing about the girls' beauty, although I thought them improved. I didn't say so; I made some little joke about Bond Street, which he pretended not to understand. So I just said I thought the girls improved, or rather were looking very pretty, and he said, "My dear mother, we must learn to look at these things from the point of view of the outsider. Place yourself in the position of a man of the world seeing them for the first time."

To begin with, Aunt Anna proceeded to explain, she could never place herself in a position to which she was not born; she did not think it right. She said that Claud then urged her to look at it from stranger's point of view, since that of man of the world was impracticable, which Aunt Anna said was a thing no mother could do, nor would she wish to do it. She left such things to actresses. Talking of actresses reminded her that Claud had even found fault with Maud as an actress, when every one knew how very excellent she was. Several newspapers, the Southshire Herald in particular, had alluded to her as one of our most talented actresses.

"We had a professional down to coach her, and he said there was really nothing he could teach her. He was a very nice man, and had all his meals with us. I went," continued Aunt Anna, "to see the great French actress who was in London in the spring, you remember? And if ever a mother went with an unprejudiced mind, I was that mother. I was prepared to think she was better than Maud, and if she had been, I should have been the first to say it. But she was not, at least not to my mind! Maud is always a lady, even on the stage, and that woman was not."

I ventured to suggest that she was perhaps not supposed to be a lady in the part. Aunt Anna said, "Perhaps not, but that does not matter; Maud would be a lady under any circumstances, whatever character she impersonated, laundress or lady. Claud says she will never act till she learns to forget herself I trust one of my daughters will never do that!"

I strove to pacify Aunt Anna, but her tender heart was wounded and she was hard to comfort.

"Claud must admire Edith's violin playing," I ventured.

Aunt Anna shook her head. "He begged me to eliminate from my mind all preconceived notions and to judge her from the unprejudiced point of view. I told Edith to put away her violin. Claud says I must call it a fiddle. I could not bear to see it. I never thought there could be such dissension in our united family."

By way of distraction, I asked if the young man at tea with the disheveled hair and startlingly unorthodox tie was a friend of Claud's, and she said, "His greatest!"

At that moment Claud came into the room, wearing a less earnest expression than usual and Aunt Anna held out a hand of forgiveness. He warmly clasped it. "Mother," he said, "Windlehurst has just told me, in strict confidence, that he considers Maud's the most beautiful face he has ever seen, except, of course, in the best period of ancient Greek art. I knew you wanted to hear the unprejudiced opinion of an unbiased outsider."

I wondered how Windlehurst would like the description! Claud went on: "I think Edith every bit as good looking, more so in some ways. Now that I have heard an unprejudiced opinion I can express mine, which you have known all along. You see, mother, people say we are a self-centered and egotistical family. I have proved that we are not."

"Dear, dearest Claud, your tie is disarranged," murmured his mother, struggling to reduce it to the dimensions of the orthodox sailor knot. "Do wait and listen to all dear Betty is telling me of dearest Pauline's wedding. So interesting. Go on, dear Betty; where had we got to?"

CHAPTER XIII

My correspondence regarding my summer plans was varied, and the suggestions contained therein numerous. Here are some of the letters.

Diana's:

> Darling Betty,—What do you say to the Cornish coast, coves, cream, and children! As much of the coast and cream, and as little of the children as you like! David has a bachelor shoot in view, and I think sea air would do the children good. I do not propose leaving any nurses at home, or sending them away; they shall all come and run after Sara should she get into the sea, when she ought not to, but you and I will have the joy of watching her. She really is delicious paddling. Think of the rocks, and the coves, and the sands, and not of the wind or of other disadvantages that may strike you. As much as you like you shall read, and whatever you like, so long as you will, at intervals, look up and smile at me. I shall love to feel you are there, so do come, not as a professional aunt, as you sometimes describe yourself, but as your own dear self.
>
> Your loving
> DIANA

Zerlina's:

> Dearest Betty,—I know how difficult you are to

find disengaged, but do try and come to Cornwall with us. The children would love to have you, and I know you enjoy tearing about after them on the sands! Nurse must go home for her holiday, and the nursery-maid is so useless. But you shall do exactly as you like. I know you wouldn't mind if I left you for a day or two. Jim is so keen that I should go to the Cross-Patches, being in the neighborhood, more or less. Do write and say you will come. I do get such headaches at the seaside, and I look so awful when I get sun burnt, but it suits you.

Yours,
ZERLINA

Julia's:

Betty dear,—You have simply got to come. Diana tells me she is asking you to Cornwall, and that, I know, you will not refuse, because for some extraordinary reason you can't refuse her anything. Oh! for Diana's charm for one day a week! What wouldn't I do! That woman wastes her life; I've always said so. But go to Cornwall, blazes, or anywhere you like, but come here on your way back—everywhere is on the way back from Cornwall. Because the house is to be full of William's friends and he is never perfectly at ease unless there is a bishop among them, and a bishop drives me to desperate deeds of wickedness. They always like me! Betty, in your capacity of professional something, think of me. I want helping more than any one. I don't ask you to give up Cornwall, but afterwards, don't disappoint your

JULIA.

A girl's:

Dear Miss Lisle,—I wonder if you will remember me. I am almost afraid to hope so. But I met you last summer at the Anstells' garden-party, and you passed me an ice, vanilla and strawberry mixed! I have never forgotten it. It was not so much passing the ice, lots of people did that, as the way you did it. I was very unhappy at the time, and there was something in your expression as you did it that made me feel you were unlike any one else I had ever met. I wore green muslin!

I am wondering whether you would come to Cornwall, to stay with us. The coast is lovely, and in its wildness one can forget one's self, and that, I think, is what one most wants to do! I know what a help you would be to me, if you could come, and I will tell you all my troubles when we have been together some days. One gets to know people by the sea very quickly, I think, don't you? Although I feel as if I had known you all my life. My hat was brown, mushroom.

Your sincere friend and admirer,
VERONICA VOKINS

P. S.—I forgot to say that my father and mother will be delighted to see you. I have ten brothers and sisters, but there is miles of coast, and I and my five sisters have a sitting-room all to ourselves. Father says "he" must pass his examinations first. I tell you this because you will then understand. "He" won the obstacle race at the Anstells', but he was in a sack, so I expect you did not notice him!

The big, sad Thomas:

Dear Miss Lisle,—For months, in fact since the day you restored the screw to my small son, I have been trying to write to you on a subject that may or may not be distasteful to you. That it will come as a surprise I feel sure. My love for my boy must be my excuse; nothing else could justify my writing to any woman as I am about to write to you. Will you be a mother to my Thomas? It would not be honest on my part to pretend that I can offer you in myself anything but a very sad and lonely man, the best of me having gone. No one could ever,—or shall ever, take the place of my beloved wife in my heart, the remains of which

I offer unreservedly to you. For the sake of my boy I am prepared to sacrifice myself, and I can at least promise you that you shall never regret by any action of mine whatever sacrifice it may entail on your part. I shall not insult you by the mention of money matters or any such things, for I feel sure that the fact of my being a rich man will make no difference in your decision as to whether or no you will be a mother to my Thomas.

Yours very sincerely,
THOMAS GLYNNE

Lady Glenburnie's:

Dear Betty,—If you should be in the North,—and why not make a certainty of it?—don't forget us! A line to say when and where to meet you is all we want, and you will find the warmest of welcomes awaiting you, and your own favorite room in the turret. Don't mention nephews or nieces in answering this.

Your affectionate
MARY GLENBURNIE

Brother Archie's:

Angel Betty,—Help a brother in distress. I'm desperately in love. First of all,—how long do you suppose it will last? Forever, I think. But I can't live at this pitch for long, and my summer plans depend on it. She is lovely. Makes me long to sing hymns on Sunday evenings; you know the kind of thing —feeling, I should say! She's like Pauline, only more beautiful, I think. I will tell you all about it when we meet. There are complications. My first trouble is this: I have taken a small place in Skye with Coningsby. Now it is perfectly impossible to live with Con when one is in love; of all the unsympathetic, dried-up old crabs, he is the worst. Now the question is, can I buy him out? Have you to stay instead, ask my beloved too, save her from drowning, which in Skye should be easy, and then live happily ever afterwards. I am consumed with a desire to save her from something. It is a symptom, I know, but, Betty dear, it is serious this time. Her eyes look as if they saw into another world, which makes me feel hopeless! I don't mind you hinting something about it to Julia, if you should see her. You needn't enter into details!

Yours ever,
ARCHIE

Of all the letters, Diana's was the most tempting.

Zerlina's had no power to lure. Dear Archie's little—he had so often written the same—sort of letters. Veronica Vokins' less, and the sad, big Thomas! What a curious letter! I hardly knew whether to laugh or to cry. How careful he was to point out the sacrifice on his part entailed in his offer. It was hardly flattering to me, except that he refrained from mentioning his worldly goods, or the advantages to me accruing from the bestowal thereof. I had at least looked unworldly when I had visited the small Thomas in bed; of that I was glad. And, after all, why should I mind? It is something, perhaps, to be asked to be a mother to a small fat Thomas. I wrote, refusing as kindly as I could. I dare say there are women who would accept the position. Let us hope, if one be found to do so, that she will not forget the mother part!

Dear Lady Glenburnie's letter had something of temptation lurking in it somewhere. The turret room, commanding its views of purple hills and sunsets, and the warmest of welcomes! But, again, the most aching of memories. I could not go there again under circumstances so different. If ever it could be again as it had been, how I should love it! So that invitation I declined, saying I should be in Cornwall with Diana. Lady Glenburnie would forgive the mention of Diana, I knew, and of Betty, Hugh, and Sara I said nothing, as she had stipulated.

Then I wrote to Julia saying I would go to her after I had been to Cornwall. She might need consoling by then, should Archie have proved himself recovered of the wounds inflicted by her. This I did not tell her. If I waited a little, there might be nothing to tell.

CHAPTER XIV

So to Cornwall I went, and found the sands and the coves and the rocks and the sea, just as Diana had said, nor was I disappointed in the back view of Sara with her petticoats tucked into her bathing-drawers. It was divine. She was delicious, too, paddling, and there were enough nurses to prevent her doing more, if necessary, and Diana and I could, if we liked, lie on the sands and watch the children. But it so happens that I love building castles and making puddings, and, curiously enough, Diana does too, and we were children once more with perhaps less hinge in our backs than formerly, but still we enjoyed ourselves immensely.

Betty, the first day, full of faith, tried to walk on the sea, and was pulled out very wet and disappointed, and her faith a little shaken, perhaps, for the moment. Hugh told her she didn't have faith hard enough. "You must go like this," and he held his breath, threatening to become purple in the face.

"Could you now?" said Betty wistfully, when Hugh was at his reddest.

"No!" he said, "because I burst. Aunt Woggles looked at me when I was just believing very hard."

Betty forgot that trouble in her infinite delight at discovering where Heaven really was. She knew if she could just row out to the silver pathway across the sea, it would lead straight to Heaven. "I know it would," she said.

Hugh objected because Heaven was in the sky, that he knew! Betty said how did he know?

"Well, look," said Hugh; "you can see it's all bright and blue and shining, and angels fly, and you can't fly on the sea, so that shows."

Betty wasn't sure of that because of flying-fish; she'd seen them in a book where "F" was for flying-fish, so she knew. But Hugh knew that angels weren't fish, because fish is good to eat and angels aren't. I was glad the culinary knowledge of Hugh and Betty didn't extend to "angels on horseback," or where should we have been in the abysses of argument?

We made expeditions which, as expeditions, were not a success. Sara objected to leaving the object of her passing affections, a starfish perhaps, and Hugh and Betty also always found treasures of their very own, which they must just watch for just a little time, in case they did something exciting. These things hinder! But still we did sometimes reach another cove, and one day, in a very secluded one, I caught sight of a pair of lovers. One can tell the most discreet of them at a glance, and more than a glance I should never have given this pair had not the girl, so much of her as I could see under a brown mushroom hat, been very pretty. Her dress too was green muslin, which was in itself compelling, and the boy with her, I felt sure, had passed no examinations. And yet they were deliriously happy, that I could tell. So the father wasn't so cruel, after all, and I doubted whether I should have been the comfort to Veronica that she had anticipated. In fact, I could easily imagine how greatly in the way I should have been. Poor professional friend! That I had at least been spared from becoming.

Veronica, no less than Betty, had discovered where Heaven really was, and the boy had a clearer definition of angels than Hugh. Hugh was right so far—they were in no way related to, or bore any resemblance to, fish. They were angels pure and simple, and the most beautiful of them, the most enchanting of them, wore a green muslin and a brown mushroom hat.

If I had been that young man, I should have objected to the dimensions of that hat, but he didn't, I suppose. Not having passed his examinations may have made a difference. He would later on, no doubt. It is a pity, perhaps, that men have to pass examinations; it robs them of much of their simplicity.

CHAPTER XV

Zerlina discovered, to her immense surprise, that she was near enough to bring all her party to play with ours, and it was arranged that she should do so on the first fine day.

It so happened that all the days were fine, so every day Diana and I watched for the small cloud in the distance that should herald their approach, and one day it appeared, no bigger than a man's hand. When it came nearer it was considerably bigger, and it finally assumed the dimensions of Zerlina, Hyacinth, the twins, Teddy, and a small nursery-maid. Betty was immensely delighted with the twins, her one ambition in life being to have twins of her own. Failing that, and every birthday only brought fresh disappointment in its wake, the care of somebody else's was the next best thing.

They really were delicious people, so round and so solemn. Hugh, for the moment, was engrossed in Teddy; Teddy having, among other things, a knife with "things in it," most of which he was mercifully unable to open. It was the certainty of being able to do so on the part of Hugh, which made him so deliriously busy. Sara was out of it, having no one as yet to play with, and she was proud and disdainful in consequence. I knew that Betty would shortly have one twin to spare, perhaps two, but this Sara could not guess, knowing nothing of twins.

"Now, Sara," I said, "we will build a castle all for our very own selves."

"Our velly, velly own selves," said Sara, hugging her spade with ecstasy. "A velly, velly big castle."

"Very, very big," I replied.

"A bemormous castle?"

"An enormous castle," I said, starting to dig the foundations.

"Dat's a velly, velly vitty hole," said Sara.

"It's going to be a castle, darling."

"For Yaya to live in?"

"Perhaps."

And Nannie and Aunt Woggles and Hugh and Betty and muvver?"

Sara danced with joy at the prospect, and Sara dancing in bathing-drawers was distracting. I dug industriously, however, and it was very hot. Sara looked on, occasionally watering the castle and me too.

"Not too much water, darling," I said, "because it makes Aunt Woggles so wet."

Sara subsided for the moment. "Is it a velly big castle?" she asked every now and then with evident anxiety.

"It's going to be, darling," I said.

"It's a velly, velly small castle now," she said sadly.

I dug harder and harder, and it seemed to me that the castle was becoming quite a respectable size, but Sara's interest had flagged.

"Aunt Woggles," she said.

"Yes, darling," I answered.

"Sall we dig a velly, velly deep hole, velly, velly deep, for all ve cwabs, and all ve vitty fish, and Nannie and Aunt Woggles?"

"A very big hole," I said; "but look at the lovely castle!"

"Yaya doesn't yike 'ollid ole castles," she said.

I began to dig a hole. One does these things, I find, for the Saras of this world, and Sara was for the moment enchanted, but it didn't last long.

"Yaya's so sirsty," she said. "Yaya wants a 'ponge cake."

"I think you would rather have some milk, darling," I said.

"Yaya's so sirsty," she said in a very sad voice. "Yaya would yike a 'ponge cake!"

"Very well, darling; but don't you want to dig any more?"

"No," she said. "Yaya doesn't yike digging."

Now was that fair?—digging, indeed, when it was the poor aunt who had been digging all the time. When I told Diana of this she shook her head and said,—Betty, it frightens me. Do you think Sara will grow up that sort of woman?"

"What sort of woman?"

"Like Polly in Charles Dudley Warner's 'My Summer in a Garden.' You remember when the husband says, 'Polly, do you know who planted that squash, or those squashes?'"

"James, I suppose."

"Well, yes, perhaps James did plant them, to a certain extent. But who hoed them?'

"We did.'"

"Well, it seems to me," I said, "that she was rather a delightful person."

"In a book, absolutely delightful. I am only thinking of Sara's husband, poor man! You see Polly's husband was an American, and that makes all the difference. You remember I told you of a man I met who in decorating his house wanted to have red walls as a background to his beautiful pictures, and his wife wanted to have green. I asked him what he did, and he said he made a compromise. I said how clever of him, how did he do it? and he said, 'We had green!' You see, Betty, what an American husband means!"

"Well, to return to Sara's, you need not worry. I think he will, in all probability, be in such raptures over the possession of anything so delicious as Sara promises to be, that he will overlook these little pluralities on her part."

"Yes, Betty, of course; but does that sort of thing last?"

"You ought to know, to a certain extent."

"Ah! but then David is such a dear."

"I think it is quite likely that Sara will find a dear too."

"I hope so, oh! how I hope so!" said Diana. "I often wonder what it must be to find you have given your daughter to some one who is unkind to her. I can hardly imagine so great a sorrow! I dare not even think of David the day Betty marries. He says he thinks it must be worse for a father than a mother."

"I wonder," I said. "I think a mother perhaps has a greater belief in the goodness of men; a woman, a happy woman certainly, has so little knowledge of men, other than her own."

"Yes," said Diana, "a good father and a good husband give one a very deep rooted faith and belief in the goodness of mankind generally. How we are prosing, Betty!"

Zerlina meanwhile sat on a rock, of the hardness of which she complained. She found fault with our cove, the sun was too hot and the wind was too strong. But then she had driven ten miles in a wagonette under Teddy and the twins, so it was no wonder she grumbled a little.

"I can't think," she said plaintively, "why my hair doesn't look nice when it blows about in the wind, and I hate myself sun burnt. I can't bear seeing my nose wherever I look. You and Betty are the stuff martyrs are made of. It would be comparatively easy to walk to the stake if you had the right amount of hair hanging down behind; without it, no amount of religious conviction would avail. Oh dear, I used to have such lots, before I had measles! I hardly knew what to do with it!"

"That's rather what we find with Betty's," said Diana; "we plait it up as tight as we can, don't we, darling?" she said, re-tying the ribbon which secured Betty's very thick pigtail.

"I had twice as much as Betty, at her age, I'm sure," said Zerlina, forgetting a photograph which stands on Jim's dressing-table, of a small fat girl with very little hair and that rather scraggy. But what does it matter? These are the sort of traditions women cling to.

Someone suggested building a steamship in the sand, grown-ups, children, and all, and Hugh was told to go and make a second-class berth. He retired to a short distance, and no sound coming from his direction, we looked round and saw him in ecstatic raptures, rocking himself backward and forward.

"What are you doing, Hugh? " we said.

"Well," said Hugh, "I was told to make a second-class berth. I suppose that means twins, and I 'm nursing them."

Zerlina took it quite well, and was easily persuaded that there was no insult intended to her twins in particular.

A few minutes later Sara appeared, triumphant, having apparently found a small child to play with.

"Who is your little friend, Sara?" I asked.

She shook her head. She didn't know, but he was delicious to play with for all that, and she bore him off in triumph.

He was not long unsought, for a young girl came anxiously towards us and said, "Have you seen a little boy?"

It reminded me a little of the story, the other way round, of a lost boy who asked a man, "Please, sir, have you seen a man without a little boy, because if you have, I'm the little boy."

She looked as anxious and as distraught as that little boy must have looked, I am sure.

"I think," said Diana, "you will find him behind that rock. —Sara," called Diana, "bring the little boy here."

A small portion of Sara's person appeared round the rock:— "We're velly busy," she said.

So rapidly do women make friendships!

"He's quite safe," said Diana; "your little brother, I suppose?"

The girl blushed. "No, I'm his mother," she said.

She looked so young and so pretty, and her hair must have

moved Zerlina to tears, it was so beautiful, and grew so prettily on her forehead. But she looked too young to be searching for lost babies all by herself.

"How old is he?" asked Diana.

"He's three," she said; then added, "his father never saw him; he went to the war soon after we were married, and he was killed. Baby is just like him," and she unfastened a miniature she wore on a chain round her neck and handed it to Diana.

I am sure Diana saw nothing but a blur, but she managed to say, "You must be glad! Come and see my little girl, she is very much the same age."

"What an extraordinarily communicative person!" said Zerlina as they walked off. "Just imagine telling strangers the whole of your history like that. I wonder if her husband left her well off."

"Can't you see he did?" I said.

"No; I don't think she is very well dressed, but you never can tell with that picturesque style of dressing. It may or may not be expensive; even that old embroidery only means probably that she had a grandmother. It is a terrible thing for a girl of that age to be left with a boy to bring up. I know, Betty, just what you are thinking—cold, heartless, mercenary Zerlina! But I'm practical."

When Diana came back, I could see in her face that she knew all about the poor little widow. It is wonderful what a comfort it seems to be even to strangers to confide in Diana. For one thing I feel sure they know that she won't tell, and that makes all the difference. It is a relief sometimes to tell some one, although some things can be better borne when nobody knows. But I imagine there was little bitterness in the sorrow of this girl widow. She too had learned something from Diana, for she turned to me and said, "Are you a relation of

Captain Lisle?"

"If his name is Archie," I said, "I am his sister."

"I've met him," and she blushed.

This, then, was the girl Archie longed to save from drowning, and who inspired him with a desire to sing hymns on Sunday evenings. Dear old Archie! I could imagine his tender, susceptible heart going out to the little widow. But I said to myself, "It's no good, Archie dear, not yet at all events, not while she looks as she does over the sea," for I was sure it was far away in a grave on the lonely veldt that her heart was buried.

"He is so devoted to children, isn't he?" she said. "He was so good to my baby. I find that men are so extraordinarily fond of children. I am afraid they will spoil him."

Whereupon the baby burst into a long dissertation on a present he had lately received. It sounded something like this: —

"Mormousman give boy a yockerile an a epelan, anye yockerile yanan yan all over de jurnmer yunder de hoha an eberelyyare."

He then proceeded to turn bead over heels, or try to, and was sharply rebuked by Sara, who rearranged his garments with stern severity, and then was about to show him the right method, when she in turn was stopped by Nannie.

One of the twins arrived at this moment to say that Hugh had called him bad names. Betty the peacemaker explained that Hugh had called him a wicket keeper, and the twin had thought he had called him a wicked keeper. So that was all right. We suggested that, in any case, the twin wasn't the best person to be wicket keeper. But he went in twice running to make up, and Hugh gave him several puddings as well. "Puddings," the nursery-maid explained, were first balls, and didn't count.

"Betty," I said, "you've got a hole in your stocking!"

"I hope it 's not a Jacob's ladder," said Betty.

"Hush, darling, hush," said Hugh; "you know we mustn't be irreverent!"

It was during an interval when we rested and drank milk and ate cake, those of us who would or could, that we discovered that the little widow was staying with a very old friend of my father's and mother's.

"And where does Lady Mary live?" asked Diana.

"Just over there. Do come and see her; she will be so delighted to see you and to show you the garden, which is quite famous."

CHAPTER XVI

The following day Diana got a delightful letter from Lady Mary asking us to go to luncheon, or to tea, or to both, or whatever we liked best, so long as it was at once, and that we stayed a long time, and brought all the children. She offered to send for us, but going in a donkey-cart was a stipulation on the part of the children, otherwise they could not or would not tear themselves away from the sand and all its fascinations. Sara was particularly offended at having to get out to tea, and more so at not being allowed to go in her bathing-drawers. But a mushroom hat trimmed with daisies appeased her, and even at that early age she saw the incongruity of that hat and those nether garments. They were packed, Hugh, Betty, Sara, and the nursery-maid, into the donkey-cart. Betty was supposed to drive, but Hugh and Sara had so large a share in the stage direction of that donkey, that I wonder we ever arrived. We did. Our approach was not dignified. The donkey would eat the lawn at the critical moment, and neither the stern rebukes of Sara, nor the gentle persuasion of Betty, had any effect; neither, to tell the truth, had the chastisements of Hugh. Of Diana's efforts and mine it is unnecessary to speak; they only made us very hot. As to Nannie, she said she would rather have ten children to deal with.

There were horribly tidy and beautifully dressed people walking about on the lawn, people who had never, I felt sure, been called upon to speak unkindly to a donkey. It was a little tactless of them, I thought, in view of our flushed cheeks, to appear so calm and cool, but they were quite kind, and I noticed that Diana as usual held a little court of her own, not entirely as the mother of Sara, either. Hugh and Betty too made friends, and hearing shouts of laughter coming from Hugh's audience, I went, aunt-like, to see what was happening, and I heard Hugh saying: —

"I've got another! What did the skeleton —"

"Hugh," I said, "I want you!"

"I'm asking riddles, Aunt Woggles."

"Yes, but have you seen the tortoise?"

The situation was saved.

I look back to the rest of that afternoon, and it is all blur and confusion. I remember the loveliness of the gardens, the peeps of distant moorland through arches of pink ramblers. I remember how the sun shone and how beautiful everything was, and above all and through all those confused memories I hear the quiet, gentle voice of Lady Mary as she talked to me of things of which I had thought no one knew anything. She asked me, I remember, if I would like to see the garden, and I loved her for her graciousness, her affection, and for her love for my mother. I could see even in the way she looked at me that it was of my mother he was thinking, and I remember, in answer to her question whether I liked the garden, saying I thought it was quite beautiful and so peaceful!

She said, "That is what I feel, the peace of it all. But you, dear Betty, are too young to feel that. It is as we grow older that the promise of peace holds out so much. But to the young, life is before them!"

All that, I remember quite clearly, and a little more. I can still see Lady Mary, so beautiful, so calm, so confident in the peace which the future held for her. Then all of a sudden came these words, "Betty, I liked your hero so much; what happened?"

It was a too sudden opening of prison doors. I was blinded by the light. I could say nothing. My secret, I felt, was wrested from me. I had ceased almost to try to hide it, it seemed so safe. What—could I say?

Lady Mary went on: "It is not from curiosity that I ask, but from a very real and deep interest. Your dear mother used so often to talk of your future. Her love for you was very wonderful, Betty."

I looked away to the purple hills and longed to escape, but she laid her hand on mine with a gentle pressure. "I liked him so much. His gentle chivalry appealed to me; it is a thing one does not meet every day. Some one, I remember, described him as being as hard as nails and full of sentiment, which was a charming description of a delightful character and a rare combination. All women, I think, would have their heroes strong, and the sentiment makes all the difference in life. If it is money, Betty dear, as I imagine it is, that must come right. It was money?"

"His father got into difficulties, no fault of his own, that—and friends made mischief."

"And he is helping his father," continued Lady Mary. "And while he is doing that, he thinks he has no right to bind a woman."

How could I say when I didn't know? "Men make that mistake; they forget how much easier it is for a woman to wait bound than to be free, not knowing. They don't distinguish between the woman who wants to get married and the woman who loves. Remember, Betty, how hard it must be for him. I am not sure that his is not the harder part."

"If he cares," I said.

"I am sure he cares," said Lady Mary softly. "There are secrets that are not mine, Betty, but there is one that is—the money shall come right. I had been looking out for a hero for some time when I met yours. This is strictly between ourselves, and you must remember that all my young people are so ludicrously well off, that an old woman doing as she likes with her own will do no one any harm. If I had had children, that, of course, would have made a difference. To me, who have lived the quiet life I have lately lived, the soldier, the man of action, appeals very strongly. Much as I love this place, it seems to me that I should love it still more if it came as quiet after a storm, a haven of rest after the battle of life."

Then she spoke of Diana. "Hers is a wonderful character, and I often think how beautiful it is that she should follow your dear mother at Hames."

"You feel that?" I said.

"Very, very strongly, dear. How happy it must have made her to feel that her grandchildren should have such a mother. I may be wrong, and you will smile at an old woman's prejudice and think that she is looking back with prejudiced eyes into that wonderful past which is always so much better than any present. I am not, but still it seems to me that Diana has something that all young people have not got nowadays, a reverence for the old, an admiration for the good, and a pity for the poor and distressed. These things take you far through life, dear, and, combined with her wonderful vitality and beauty, make her a power.

"Talking of your beautiful mother, it was said years ago that she was the only woman of whom I had ever been jealous. I am old enough to tell you these things. It is the privilege of the old to enlist the sympathies of the young! But it was not true. I had every reason to be jealous, as had most women I ever saw, but jealousy in connection with anything so perfect as your mother, I think, was not possible. Her beauty was of the kind which disarms jealousy. It was beyond comparison or criticism. It seemed to belong to another world, and yet she was so tender to the sinners, so understanding, so full of loving kindness. Hers was a beauty of the soul as well as the body, and that beauty is as remote from the everyday prettiness as the earth is from the stars. Her expression had something of the divine in it, as if she had seen God face to face. I see the same look coming in Diana's face. Old Sir George used to say it would be worth committing a sin to be forgiven by your mother. He said her look was a benediction."

As I said good-by to Lady Mary, she held my hand and said, "Betty dear, you will some day forgive an interfering old woman, and in days to come, when you look to these distant hills, you will remember this day with a kind thought for your beautiful mother's old friend."

"Isn't Lady Mary a darling?" said Diana, as we walked home through the scented lanes on that most wonderful of summer evenings. "You look as if you had been seeing visions, Betty, quite dazed like, as Nannie used to say."

"I often see visions," I said.

"Have you been crying, Aunt Woggles?" said Hugh. "Were all the peaches gone when you got back?"

Betty slipped her little hand into mine. "You promised to let me walk with you for a little. Shall we pick honeysuckle, supposing we see any?"

"Yes, we will, darling."

"Supposing you can't reach it," she said.

"There is always some within reach."

"I suppose grown-ups can always reach things," said Betty.

Later, in the quiet darkness of the night, I could picture the garden, the roses, the distant moor, Lady Mary's beautiful face, but I could not bring myself to believe that I had really heard those words, "I am sure that he cares."

Surely I had dreamed them, or Lady Mary had, because if they were true, why had he said nothing? How should he have told her what he could not tell me?

Mary C.E. Wemyss

CHAPTER XVII

Then came that wonderful morning on which I read that Captain Paul Buchanan was coming home, was expected to arrive that very day. I opened the paper at breakfast, as usual and my eyes caught the word that at any time had the power to set my heart thumping and to send the blood rushing to my head, a word common enough, and which to most people, beyond relating to a country always interesting, means little— Africa. It is curious that a day that is to change the whole of one's life should begin exactly like any other day. Of the most important things we have no premonition, most of us.

That what I longed and prayed for every hour of my life should come to pass was not wonderful, but that a day on which I was to be called to make the greatest sacrifice of my life should steal stealthily upon me seems strange.

That morning when I came downstairs, my little house in Chelsea looked exactly like it always had done. The sun shone as the sun does shine in the early winter in London, and no more, until after I had read that paragraph; then, behold a new world was born. Why had my eyes been blind to the gloriousness of the morning? Why had I thought the day an ordinarily dull one with just the amount of pale sunshine which is meted out to those happy people who are wise enough to live within easy reach of the river? Yes, I know, some people do say that Chelsea is foggy.

It depends so much on their lives. No place could be foggy to me that day. My fear was that Nannie should read the news in my face. I looked away when she said, "Anything in the paper?" as she had said a hundred times before. She always came to see me eat my breakfast, so she said, but I knew it was really to hear the news. I handed her the paper, although I hated to let the words out of my sight, and she glanced at it. She paused and walked to the window. Kind Nannie, she was giving me time. She blew her nose, she was crying, she knew. A double knock at the door brought my heart to a standstill. Lady Mary was right, he did care. It seemed hours before the telegram was brought to me. I hardly dared to open it. There is some happiness too great to bear. I opened it and read: —

Sara very ill. Come at once.

DIANA

"Nannie," I said, "I am going to Hames."

"To-day?" she said. She knew it was my day of days.

"I must, Nannie. Will you come?"

"No; I'll stay here. Poor Mrs. David, whatever will she do?"

I could hardly imagine, and I am glad to remember that my sorrow seemed a small thing compared to hers.

It would be impossible for me to describe that journey. The train crept along. It seemed to stop hours at the station. No one seemed to remember that Sara was ill. I felt the grip of a cold hand on my heart. Should I ever arrive? I did at last, and found a groom waiting for me at the station, with a dogcart. His mouth twitched, and he could hardly control his voice to tell me that there was no fresh news. The carriages were wanted for the doctors; did I mind the dogcart? Mind? I could have urged the horse to a gallop, and yet I dreaded to arrive.

It was strange to pass through the quiet, deserted hall, up the stairs, and to hear no sound. A nurse opened a door and spoke in a whisper. I went into the room, and not until I saw Diana, so lovely in her grief, did I realize the agony of her suffering. She put out her hand and silently pressed mine. I turned away so that she should not see my face.

A man, a stranger to me, sat by the bedside, his eyes fixed on the child lying there. He was the great London doctor, in whom I could see all hope was centered. There were other doctors and nurses, I believe, but it all seemed confusion to me now; but poor, broken hearted Nannie I remember. She stood at a distance. Not a sound was uttered, and I took up my watch with the others, to watch that precious life ebbing away. The soft flitting backward and forward of nurses, a word now and then from the great man who held not only the life of Sara in his hands, but, it seemed to me, the life of my beautiful Diana, only broke the intense silence. The night came on and we still watched.

The doctor's face became sterner and graver and the little life weaker, or so it seemed to me. Diana knelt at the side of the bed. She never moved.

As the dawn broke, Sara opened her eyes and said, "Nannie."

Diana rose and beckoned to Nannie. Nannie hesitated, and Diana, taking her hand, whispered, "Dear Nannie, I am so glad," and gave up her place. It is not given to all of us to reach great heights, but Diana at that moment, I think, reached the divine in human nature. Then came the moment, too wonderful to think of, when the doctor told Diana that the great danger was over.

Later he said to David, "My boy, you have given your children the greatest of all blessings in their mother. Thank God for her every moment of your life. I've seen many mothers and many sick children, but—thank God, and don't forget it."

Dear David, I think most of us thank God oftener than we

know and in many and divers ways, and I am not sure that David does not do it every time he looks at Diana.

CHAPTER XVIII

Sara, having got over the crisis and being on the fair road to recovery,—children recover quickly,—my heart turned towards home—and a longing to get back obsessed me. I could think of nothing but home, now that Diana's immediate need of me was over. She begged me to stay with her. To fail her at such a moment was a great grief to me, but I could make no further sacrifice. I must go home.

"I must go, David," I urged.

"Of course, if you must, you must, Betty, but I should have thought after all Diana has gone through, you would have stayed with her. You have always been so much to each other."

How he hurt me, as if I wouldn't do anything in the world for Diana; but I must go home.

"David," I said in desperation, "I must go. If I promise to come back directly, you won't misunderstand my going?"

"I'll try to understand, Betty, that you have some very strong reason for going back."

"Thank you, David," I said.

"But," he continued, "you must tell Diana yourself."

I went to her room, where she was lying down. "Diana,

darling," I said, "I want very much to go home, if only for a day."

"Of course, Betty, you must go. But don't look so distressed. I must have been selfish if I gave you the impression that I would not let you go. It is only that I love so having you, you are such a rock, and oh! it seems like some awful and terrible dream we have been through, doesn't it? Sara asked for her darling bunny today. Think what that means! Darling Betty, I pray that some great happiness may come to you some day. I begin to believe that the greatest joys come through the greatest sorrows."

"Don't, Diana," I whispered. "I can't bear you to be too kind. I suppose it's all we've been through, but I feel."

"I know, Betty," she whispered. "I lie here too tired to do anything but thank God. I ache with thankfulness, for you among other blessings. Come back soon."

"What did Diana say?" asked David, who was waiting outside the door. "Did she understand?"

"Understand? Did you ever know a time when Diana didn't understand?"

I went. Oh, the joy of setting out towards home! That ridiculously small house in Chelsea in which were centered all my hopes. Some word might be there waiting for me. Nannie might have thought nothing of sufficient importance to forward at such a moment. How I hoped that was it, and that it might be there, else all my hopes were shattered.

I opened the door with my latchkey. I looked. No telegram lay on the table; that I saw at a glance. Then Nannie appeared. She was crying.

"Nannie," I said, "don't cry, she is much better, and is going to get quite well; only I had to come home."

How explain to Nannie that I had left Sara and Diana at such a moment!

"Your bat's crooked," said Nannie.

"You ridiculous old person," I said, "what does that matter?" Nannie sniffed. I put my hat straight. "Is that better?"

"Yes, it's better, it'll do," she answered, not quite satisfied, evidently. I wondered why she asked no questions. Why had I come home to this? No wonder David had been surprised at my leaving Diana! What was the use?

Then Nannie said with a startling suddenness, "Some one is waiting for you upstairs."

"Someone for me, Nannie. What do you mean?"

"He's waiting," she said, between laughter and sobs. "He's waiting."

I often wonder how I had the strength to go upstairs and open the door. But I did, and there surely enough he stood, only a few feet of green-painted boards separating us. How I crossed them I never knew. He came halfway, no doubt.

I should never have done the journey alone, and I wondered too how it was we met as lovers! That was the most wonderful part of all. How, when I did not even know that he cared, could it have happened? It was all too wonderful, and I was too dazed with happiness to question anything at the moment. I only knew that the world had become a paradise, and that the past years of doubt and perplexity had fallen away like a disused garment.

Then we began to talk, and the mystery deepened. He spoke of a telegram. I had never received one! And my telegram? I had never sent one! He laughed, and when I said I didn't understand, he said what was the use of understanding when knowing was sufficient?

It was all very puzzling, but I was content. There was so much to talk of, so many explanations to make and to hear! But in time we came back to the telegram. There had been no such thing!

He laughed. "I have it here," he said, putting his hand on his coat-pocket.

"Show it to me," I pleaded.

Never; it was his, and his alone.

"But nothing is yours now that is not mine," I urged, "at least, if you have asked me to marry you."

"Betty," he said, "I quite forgot. I came home for the express purpose of doing so. I have thought and dreamed of nothing else, all through the long marches in Africa; all the way home I have thought of that and of your answer. Betty, will you marry me?"

"I shall be delighted, Captain Buchanan. But where is my telegram to you, your telegram to me?"

It I think Nannie must have one."

"And did she answer it? Oh, what did she say?"

"Never mind; she said exactly the right thing. Don't let's discuss Nannie's telegram when we have to make up for the silence of years! 0 Betty! shall I wake up?"

A little later he said, "Tell me, did you care that night at the Frasers'?"

"I said I never remembered a time when I didn't care.

"0 Betty! if only you hadn't been so proud!"

"Or you so horribly unununderstandable!"

CHAPTER XIX

You wonderful Nannie," I said later, as I sat at her feet, "how did you do it?"

"Quite easily," said Nannie. "When I saw that you must go to Hames, as of course you had to, I thought to myself, I'll wait! Years ago my lady said to me, I Nannie, don't let my child throw away her own chance of happiness. I feel that a day may come when she will be called upon to make a sacrifice, and she will make it, regardless of her own feelings. You were always giving up your toys and things to the boys; that's what made your mother think of it. The day she spoke of came the morning the telegram came from Hames. I had been waiting and waiting so as to be sure to do what your mother told me, and the day came. You see, I saw the paper, and I knew!"

"How, Nannie? No one knew, I thought."

"Ah, nannies know things; much use they'd be in this world if they didn't? I know lots of things I'm not supposed to! Well, I waited, and no telegram came from him that day. There were all sorts of things about him in the evening paper, being a hero and a lion and all those sort of things. Then the next day the telegram came. The ship had been late; you never can tell with ships. Leave ships to sailors, I say. Well, I opened the telegram. It said, 'Will you see me if I come straight to you ?' or some such words, and I answered it."

"What did you say, Nannie?"

Mary C.E. Wemyss

"I don't see that that matters. There's nothing in words, and I'm no scholar."

"Nannie dear, it does matter. It meant everything in the world to me. If only you knew how happy I am, how ridiculously happy."

"It's all right, then. I've done what she said." A rapturous smile illuminated her old face.

"All right, Nannie?"

Only a hug can express some things. Nannie straightened her cap. "Well, then," she said, drawing herself up, "I couldn't do it for sixpence, it cost ninepence halfpenny. I said, 'Come. Been waiting for you for years.'"

"Nannie!" I exclaimed.

Choose from Thousands of 1stWorldLibrary Classics By

A. M. Barnard
Ada Leverson
Adolphus William Ward
Aesop
Agatha Christie
Alexander Aaronsohn
Alexander Kielland
Alexandre Dumas
Alfred Gatty
Alfred Ollivant
Alice Duer Miller
Alice Turner Curtis
Alice Dunbar
Allen Chapman
Alleyne Ireland
Ambrose Bierce
Amelia E. Barr
Amory H. Bradford
Andrew Lang
Andrew McFarland Davis
Andy Adams
Angela Brazil
Anna Alice Chapin
Anna Sewell
Annie Besant
Annie Hamilton Donnell
Annie Payson Call
Annie Roe Carr
Annonaymous
Anton Chekhov
Archibald Lee Fletcher
Arnold Bennett
Arthur C. Benson
Arthur Conan Doyle
Arthur M. Winfield
Arthur Ransome
Arthur Schnitzler
Arthur Train
Atticus
B.H. Baden-Powell
B. M. Bower
B. C. Chatterjee
Baroness Emmuska Orczy
Baroness Orczy
Basil King
Bayard Taylor
Ben Macomber
Bertha Muzzy Bower
Bjornstjerne Bjornson

Booth Tarkington
Boyd Cable
Bram Stoker
C. Collodi
C. E. Orr
C. M. Ingleby
Carolyn Wells
Catherine Parr Traill
Charles A. Eastman
Charles Amory Beach
Charles Dickens
Charles Dudley Warner
Charles Farrar Browne
Charles Ives
Charles Kingsley
Charles Klein
Charles Hanson Towne
Charles Lathrop Pack
Charles Romyn Dake
Charles Whibley
Charles Willing Beale
Charlotte M. Braeme
Charlotte M. Yonge
Charlotte Perkins Stetson
Clair W. Hayes
Clarence Day Jr.
Clarence E. Mulford
Clemence Housman
Confucius
Coningsby Dawson
Cornelis DeWitt Wilcox
Cyril Burleigh
D. H. Lawrence
Daniel Defoe
David Garnett
Dinah Craik
Don Carlos Janes
Donald Keyhoe
Dorothy Kilner
Dougan Clark
Douglas Fairbanks
E. Nesbit
E. P. Roe
E. Phillips Oppenheim
E. S. Brooks
Earl Barnes
Edgar Rice Burroughs
Edith Van Dyne
Edith Wharton

Edward Everett Hale
Edward J. O'Biren
Edward S. Ellis
Edwin L. Arnold
Eleanor Atkins
Eleanor Hallowell Abbott
Eliot Gregory
Elizabeth Gaskell
Elizabeth McCracken
Elizabeth Von Arnim
Ellem Key
Emerson Hough
Emilie F. Carlen
Emily Bronte
Emily Dickinson
Enid Bagnold
Enilor Macartney Lane
Erasmus W. Jones
Ernie Howard Pie
Ethel May Dell
Ethel Turner
Ethel Watts Mumford
Eugene Sue
Eugenie Foa
Eugene Wood
Eustace Hale Ball
Evelyn Everett-green
Everard Cotes
F. H. Cheley
F. J. Cross
F. Marion Crawford
Fannie E. Newberry
Federick Austin Ogg
Ferdinand Ossendowski
Fergus Hume
Florence A. Kilpatrick
Fremont B. Deering
Francis Bacon
Francis Darwin
Frances Hodgson Burnett
Frances Parkinson Keyes
Frank Gee Patchin
Frank Harris
Frank Jewett Mather
Frank L. Packard
Frank V. Webster
Frederic Stewart Isham
Frederick Trevor Hill
Frederick Winslow Taylor

Friedrich Kerst
Friedrich Nietzsche
Fyodor Dostoyevsky
G.A. Henty
G.K. Chesterton
Gabrielle E. Jackson
Garrett P. Serviss
Gaston Leroux
George A. Warren
George Ade
Geroge Bernard Shaw
George Cary Eggleston
George Durston
George Ebers
George Eliot
George Gissing
George MacDonald
George Meredith
George Orwell
George Sylvester Viereck
George Tucker
George W. Cable
George Wharton James
Gertrude Atherton
Gordon Casserly
Grace E. King
Grace Gallatin
Grace Greenwood
Grant Allen
Guillermo A. Sherwell
Gulielma Zollinger
Gustav Flaubert
H. A. Cody
H. B. Irving
H.C. Bailey
H. G. Wells
H. H. Munro
H. Irving Hancock
H. R. Naylor
H. Rider Haggard
H. W. C. Davis
Haldeman Julius
Hall Caine
Hamilton Wright Mabie
Hans Christian Andersen
Harold Avery
Harold McGrath
Harriet Beecher Stowe
Harry Castlemon
Harry Coghill
Harry Houidini

Hayden Carruth
Helent Hunt Jackson
Helen Nicolay
Hendrik Conscience
Hendy David Thoreau
Henri Barbusse
Henrik Ibsen
Henry Adams
Henry Ford
Henry Frost
Henry James
Henry Jones Ford
Henry Seton Merriman
Henry W Longfellow
Herbert A. Giles
Herbert Carter
Herbert N. Casson
Herman Hesse
Hildegard G. Frey
Homer
Honore De Balzac
Horace B. Day
Horace Walpole
Horatio Alger Jr.
Howard Pyle
Howard R. Garis
Hugh Lofting
Hugh Walpole
Humphry Ward
Ian Maclaren
Inez Haynes Gillmore
Irving Bacheller
Isabel Cecilia Williams
Isabel Hornibrook
Israel Abrahams
Ivan Turgenev
J.G.Austin
J. Henri Fabre
J. M. Barrie
J. M. Walsh
J. Macdonald Oxley
J. R. Miller
J. S. Fletcher
J. S. Knowles
J. Storer Clouston
J. W. Duffield
Jack London
Jacob Abbott
James Allen
James Andrews
James Baldwin

James Branch Cabell
James DeMille
James Joyce
James Lane Allen
James Lane Allen
James Oliver Curwood
James Oppenheim
James Otis
James R. Driscoll
Jane Abbott
Jane Austen
Jane L. Stewart
Janet Aldridge
Jens Peter Jacobsen
Jerome K. Jerome
Jessie Graham Flower
John Buchan
John Burroughs
John Cournos
John F. Kennedy
John Gay
John Glasworthy
John Habberton
John Joy Bell
John Kendrick Bangs
John Milton
John Philip Sousa
John Taintor Foote
Jonas Lauritz Idemil Lie
Jonathan Swift
Joseph A. Altsheler
Joseph Carey
Joseph Conrad
Joseph E. Badger Jr
Joseph Hergesheimer
Joseph Jacobs
Jules Vernes
Julian Hawthrone
Julie A Lippmann
Justin Huntly McCarthy
Kakuzo Okakura
Karle Wilson Baker
Kate Chopin
Kenneth Grahame
Kenneth McGaffey
Kate Langley Bosher
Kate Langley Bosher
Katherine Cecil Thurston
Katherine Stokes
L. A. Abbot
L. T. Meade

L. Frank Baum
Latta Griswold
Laura Dent Crane
Laura Lee Hope
Laurence Housman
Lawrence Beasley
Leo Tolstoy
Leonid Andreyev
Lewis Carroll
Lewis Sperry Chafer
Lilian Bell
Lloyd Osbourne
Louis Hughes
Louis Joseph Vance
Louis Tracy
Louisa May Alcott
Lucy Fitch Perkins
Lucy Maud Montgomery
Luther Benson
Lydia Miller Middleton
Lyndon Orr
M. Corvus
M. H. Adams
Margaret E. Sangster
Margret Howth
Margaret Vandercook
Margaret W. Hungerford
Margret Penrose
Maria Edgeworth
Maria Thompson Daviess
Mariano Azuela
Marion Polk Angellotti
Mark Overton
Mark Twain
Mary Austin
Mary Catherine Crowley
Mary Cole
Mary Hastings Bradley
Mary Roberts Rinehart
Mary Rowlandson
M. Wollstonecraft Shelley
Maud Lindsay
Max Beerbohm
Myra Kelly
Nathaniel Hawthrone
Nicolo Machiavelli
O. F. Walton
Oscar Wilde

Owen Johnson
P.G. Wodehouse
Paul and Mabel Thorne
Paul G. Tomlinson
Paul Severing
Percy Brebner
Percy Keese Fitzhugh
Peter B. Kyne
Plato
Quincy Allen
R. Derby Holmes
R. L. Stevenson
R. S. Ball
Rabindranath Tagore
Rahul Alvares
Ralph Bonehill
Ralph Henry Barbour
Ralph Victor
Ralph Waldo Emmerson
Rene Descartes
Ray Cummings
Rex Beach
Rex E. Beach
Richard Harding Davis
Richard Jefferies
Richard Le Gallienne
Robert Barr
Robert Frost
Robert Gordon Anderson
Robert L. Drake
Robert Lansing
Robert Lynd
Robert Michael Ballantyne
Robert W. Chambers
Rosa Nouchette Carey
Rudyard Kipling
Saint Augustine
Samuel B. Allison
Samuel Hopkins Adams
Sarah Bernhardt
Sarah C. Hallowell
Selma Lagerlof
Sherwood Anderson
Sigmund Freud
Standish O'Grady
Stanley Weyman
Stella Benson
Stella M. Francis

Stephen Crane
Stewart Edward White
Stijn Streuvels
Swami Abhedananda
Swami Parmananda
T. S. Ackland
T. S. Arthur
The Princess Der Ling
Thomas A. Janvier
Thomas A Kempis
Thomas Anderton
Thomas Bailey Aldrich
Thomas Bulfinch
Thomas De Quincey
Thomas Dixon
Thomas H. Huxley
Thomas Hardy
Thomas More
Thornton W. Burgess
U. S. Grant
Upton Sinclair
Valentine Williams
Various Authors
Vaughan Kester
Victor Appleton
Victor G. Durham
Victoria Cross
Virginia Woolf
Wadsworth Camp
Walter Camp
Walter Scott
Washington Irving
Wilbur Lawton
Wilkie Collins
Willa Cather
Willard F. Baker
William Dean Howells
William le Queux
W. Makepeace Thackeray
William W. Walter
William Shakespeare
Winston Churchill
Yei Theodora Ozaki
Yogi Ramacharaka
Young E. Allison
Zane Grey

www.ingramcontent.com/pod-product-compliance
Lightning Source LLC
Chambersburg PA
CBHW051849170626
46807CB00003B/1404